BACKDROP TO MURDER

A LANIE PRICE MYSTERY

PERSIA WALKER

BLOOD VINTAGE
NEW YORK • MUNICH

THANK YOU

Jordan Walker • Tyler-Marie Walker
Debra Jones • Felicia Chambers
Cassandra Foley • Maggie Covington
Tara Dolan Wright • Radiah Hubbert
Classy Green • Jane T. Aptaker

ABOUT THIS BOOK

On a dank night in September, reporter Lanie Price is called to the scene of a grisly double murder. The victims: a popular photographer and a Cotton Club beauty. The suspect: the dead man's jealous wife.

Driven by a promise to the families of the victims, Lanie delves deeper into the case. She finds her leads evaporating and her eyes opened to the possibility of a serial killer at work.

Backdrop to Murder is the latest book in the Lanie Price mystery series. If you like suspense combined with nostalgia, then you'll love this 1920's noir mystery.

PROLOGUE

Y ou ever heard of the colored photographer Andrew King? Never did? Well, that's a damn shame. But in a way, it would've surprised me if you had. Not many people remember his name nowadays, but a lot more would've—if he'd survived.

As a young man still in his twenties, Andrew was more than making his way. He was giving that guy with the Dutch name a run for his money. You know the one. James Van Der Zee. He's famous now. Took a load of pictures of Harlem hot-shots: Florence Mills, Hazel Scott, and the like. Don't get me wrong. Van Der Zee was something all right. But the way people talk, you'd think he was the only colored man taking pictures in Harlem back then; that just wasn't so.

There was a man named Woodard—William E. Woodard —and a couple of guys by the name of Vernon and King on West 135th, and Walter Baker, up on 133rd and Lenox. There was even a woman, Winfred Hall. She and her husband ran an institute that taught photography.

Then, there was Andrew.

I was a reporter for the *Harlem Chronicle*. That little paper kept up with all the doings in Harlem. It was a weekly and it was hot. We knew who was doing what, where and with whom. But to say it was all gossip would be unfair. This was a legitimate paper and we dished out any social news that was fit to print.

I had my own column, a little slice of life called "Lanie's World," sort of a paper within the paper. My photo ran with it, and I got to pick and choose what I wanted to write. I'd just finished covering the Joplin murder trial when the King story broke and I jumped on it.

Brandy Sullivan was one of those *café au lait* chorines you always heard tell about. "Tall, tan and terrific," she was the lead dancer in the nightly floor show at the Cotton Club. She had grown up in the tobacco fields of Virginia, then come up North to the big city and made good. All was going well for Brandy, till the night she met a pit bull by the name of Big Earl, and up and married him.

Big Earl was a prizefighter, heavyweight division. He was also an albino. The white folks didn't know what to make of him, this giant black man with milky white skin, but the colored folk loved him. He didn't have the elegance of Jack Johnson or the charm of Tiger Flowers, but he did pack a mean right uppercut. He was hot-headed, brash and jealous. He knew not to threaten white men if they came on to Brandy, but he'd deck a colored man in a second.

Which brings us back to Andrew.

Rumor had it that Brandy had fallen for him. You see, Andrew wasn't just talented. He was fine, one of the finest men I have ever seen, and I've seen a'plenty. To top it off, he didn't seem to know just how fine he was. He was a good man, thoughtful, funny and kind—had a heart as big as a mountain. Legions of people were in love with him, most of them women, but more than a few men could've been counted in there, too.

To Andrew, that was all just bunkum. It meant nothing. He had his love, his "one true love," and that was his wife, Tessie. She was talented, too. Her collection of essays, *The Bitter Herbs of May*, had drawn rave reviews. I had read it, and loved it. Tessie, it seemed, was one of those rare, gifted writers whose work appealed to both the critic and the general public.

Unfortunately, Tessie herself didn't appeal to either one. She was reserved, socially awkward and beyond plain. I had spoken to her only briefly before the events I'm about to relate, and that was at a party she'd attended with Andrew. She had seemed out of place. She was tall and thin and about as curvy as a pencil. So, she actually had the perfect figure for the times we lived in. But she had a way of dressing like a middle-aged spinster and those thick spectacles she had propped on her nose didn't help.

Rumor had it that she was every bit as smart and perceptive as the esteemed W. E. B. DuBois. Having read her work, I didn't doubt it. But she was a woman, and an unfashionable one at that, living in a society that valued beauty over brains, silliness over sanity. So, she got no kudos for her intelligence, only darts for her dullness.

In point of fact, a lot of folk didn't think Tessie made a fitting wife for such a fine-looking man. I remember hearing them whispering at that party, talking about her as she and I walked by.

"Hmm-hmph! Just what does he see in her?"

And they weren't whispering all that softly, either. If I heard them, then she must've heard them, too.

Nevertheless, for a while there, it looked as though they both were going to be stars. Andrew was making marks as a photographer and Tessie, popular or not, was destined for a place at the top, right up there with Zora Neale Hurston, Nella Larson and Jessie Fauset, on the vanguard of Harlem literati.

But all that changed one bleak September night, and all it took was a bullet—two to be exact.

1

It was ten minutes after midnight when my telephone rang, interrupting what promised to be a lovely night with the man of my choosing.

He sat propped up in bed with thick white pillows behind him. His bronze skin glowed in the dancing light from my bedroom fireplace. The only item he was wearing was the cologne I'd given him for his birthday, and the white sheets that pooled around his waist.

He was a good-looking man, and a tender and generous lover. The last thing I wanted to be doing was leaving him alone in that big warm bed.

It had been a long day, and an even longer evening at a social club meeting. I'd tried to hide my impatience; these clubs and the women who ran them were my bread and butter, my being a society reporter and all. Normally, I enjoyed the meetings. Some of these ladies were incredibly smart and entrepreneurial. But that evening, I couldn't wait to get out of there. Couldn't wait to be with him. We were looking forward to a luscious night.

So, when the phone jangled, I tried to ignore it. But when

the ring got so shrill, the phone looked about to jump off the hook, I snatched it up. What the caller told me totally killed the mood. Fifteen minutes later, I was dressed. I kissed lover a temporary good-bye, said I'd see him in the morning, and jumped into my car, speeding from my Strivers' Row townhouse down to 122nd Street.

I didn't want to believe what I'd been told. Andrew seemed like the most unlikely of victims. He was popular and so easy to get along with. Everybody wanted him to take their picture. Everybody trusted him to make them look good, unforgettably good.

He had a studio on Lenox Avenue, midway up the block between 122nd and 123rd, in the half-basement of a three-story brownstone. I remember the day my late husband, Hamp, and I went to see him, the day Andrew ended up taking the only decent picture I had of me and Hamp together.

Andrew had been so proud. He'd just hung his new sign over the door: "King's Photography Studio," it said, with a blurb beneath it that read, "Every customer is treated like royalty." He'd pointed it out to us, folded his arms across his chest and beamed with pride. Clearly, he was a man with a vision, a sense of where he wanted to go and how he meant to get there.

It was hard to accept that that vision would never be fully realized.

I parked my motorcar on the corner of 122nd, in front of the still-lit windows of Darleen's Fish 'n' Fry, and hurried through the chilly night, sidestepping puddles. You could see the studio from afar. The cops had turned on all the lights, so the place was aglow, the lights reflected in the puddles on the sidewalk.

The newspaper stand across the street was shuttered and dark. This street was mostly residential, but a couple of small restaurants broke the monotony, and a slew of nightclubs stood around the corner. The clubs always brought foot traffic. On this night, they had brought a throng to the studio's door.

The crowd was at least five-people deep, thickly knotted and clogging the entrance. I excused and elbowed my way through. The entrance was three steps down from the sidewalk, sandwiched between steps leading up to the brownstone's front door on the left and the boarded-up street entrance to a defunct grocery store on the right.

At the head of the steps, a young patrolman put up a hand to bar the way. I held up my press ID. He looked unsure, then relented and let me through. I hurried down the cracked and worn concrete steps. The front door was open. I stepped inside and slowed to a halt.

After the chill outside, it felt incredibly warm soon the inside, warm and stuffy. Men in uniforms and men in white, filled the small space just inside the entryway, in front of the cash register, the counter, and displays of religious bric-a-brac. They moved in a busy stream that flowed from the back to the front, and back again. From the rear, where Andrew had his studio, came the wretched sound of a woman weeping and a man's voice, trying to calm her down.

I shouldered my way to the back, only to be blocked by another patrolman, this one older and tougher than the last.

"Nah, nah. You can't come in here." He waved me away.

"It's all right. I'm a reporter." I flashed my press card.

He raised an eyebrow. "A colored reporter?" he asked, "Is there really such a thing? Oh, go on with you and stop waving that silly card in my face. What do you take me for?"

"Reilly, let her in," said a voice from inside.

It was the Irish brogue of Detective John Blackie, from Homicide. He and I had known each other for years, going back to when I was working the crime beat at the *Harlem Age*.

Reilly stiffened and his lips tightened in resentment.

"He said to let me in," I told him.

For a moment, it looked as though he was going to be dumb and defy orders. But he must've thought better of it, because he did the smart thing and stepped aside.

* * *

Andrew's studio was a magical place. From the Victorian chairs and Edwardian tables to the leather-bound books and grand piano; from the faux fireplaces, Greek columns, and gothic gates, to the moose head on one wall, it was magic, magic everywhere. Clothing racks stood in the corner, draped with finery that ranged from canes and top hats to homburgs, trilbies, and fedoras for the male customers, to necklaces, pearls, and feather boas for the female.

The walls themselves were a sight to behold, painted with floor-to-ceiling murals that evoked moods and fantasies. The "moon over water" appeared sweet and romantic; the "villa garden" was genteel. In this room, you could go anywhere, be anyone, and pay to have the illusion preserved in black and white.

All that whimsy. Gone now. Stripped away. Violence had turned the murals into backdrops to murder.

"I'm so sorry, baby. Please, forgive me. Please."

The weeping had faded. There was only the sound of a broken whisper and the repeated babbling of words of regret.

"So sorry. So, so, sorry. Please, please, forgive me! Please!"

A police photographer had set up a triangle of tall, thin tripods and suspended a camera overhead. Under the harsh glare of his lights, the scene was grisly, surreal.

Two figures lay at the center of the spotlight, contorted and still, united by a pool of blood. Sprinkled with bits of brain matter and skull, the blood had sprayed across the floor and laced the lower part of the wall behind them.

Brandy Sullivan lay on her back, her right arm flung back, her right leg folded beneath her. Her upper torso was partially blocked from view by the thin man crouched over her: Doc Winslow, from the medical examiner's office.

Andrew lay alongside her, his arms splayed, both knees bent. Tessie sat next to him, cradling his head. She caressed his face, weeping, and whispering over and over again, "I didn't mean it, baby. I didn't mean it. God knows, I didn't. Please, don't leave me, please."

Blackie was squatting next to her, urging her to let them examine Andrew, but she shook her head. She clung to her dead husband. She wasn't about to let go.

Blackie glanced up at me, just long enough to acknowledge my presence with a nod, then beckoned the nearest patrolman to come and help him. Together, they grabbed Tessie up under her arms and pulled her to her feet. Winslow quickly moved to bend over Andrew. Tessie gave one last wail, buried her face in Blackie's chest, and sobbed, shoulders heaving.

"Now, now, Mrs. King." He patted her on the back. "Ease on up, lassie. Ease on up. We're going to have to ask you some questions now. Understand?"

She raised her head, wiped her eyes with the back of her hand, and nodded.

Briefly, I thought he might question her in my presence. But no such luck. Instead, he handed her over to the patrolman with the instruction to take her to the station.

As I watched the officer lead her away, I heard her words over and over again. Confession words. Could she have really done this? Had she?

Blackie's hard gaze met mine. It was pretty damn clear what he was thinking.

I returned my attention to Andrew and Brandy.

They had died hard. The bullet had punched through his right eye. Orange-brown lesions dotted his face—burn marks from having been gunned down at close range. The three middle fingers of his right hand were gone. Shot off. He'd probably held up his hand to defend himself.

Then, there was Brandy.

She'd been beautiful, once. Now, her lips were scorched and blackened; her teeth broken and exposed and crusted with blood. The physical damage was bad enough, but it was her expression that got me. It was her eyes. They were open and staring, frozen in a rictus of terror. Her mascara was smeared and her makeup streaked by trails of tears. She must have wept, must've begged for her life.

"You gonna throw up?" Blackie asked, suddenly standing at my side.

"You know me better than that."

But I was, in fact, having a hard time keeping my dinner down. This wasn't my first murder scene. Far from it. I'd covered a good number when working as a crime reporter, but I'd never gotten used to them. And the fact that this one involved someone I knew, someone I liked and admired ...

Blackie hitched his trousers and crouched down next to Winslow. "You got anything for me?"

The medical examiner removed his wire-rimmed spectacles, squeezed the bridge of his nose, then slipped them back on again. His eyes were red-rimmed and tired.

"I'd say death occurred sometime within the last two hours. The apparent cause in both cases was a gunshot to the head. With the man, it was to the right eye; the shooter just aimed and fired. With her," he sighed, "it was a bit different."

He took her lower lip and pulled it down, exposing the damage. "You see here," he pointed to the inner lining of the lip. "The mucosal hemorrhaging? It's an indicator of externally induced pressure. You can practically see the impressions left by the gun."

"In other words," Blackie muttered, "the killer shoved the gun right up against her mouth, then pulled the trigger."

Winslow sighed. "I've never seen anything like it. Homicidal shootings through the mouth are rare. Whoever did this, they really had it in for her."

"You're sure this wasn't a murder-suicide?" I asked.

Blackie shot me a look. He knew that for anyone accused in this case, murder-suicide would be the most likely line of defense.

"You mean, as in she shot him and then shot herself?" Winslow asked.

"Or vice versa," I said, even though I found either way hard to imagine.

"No," Winslow shook his head. "Not likely." He held up two fingers and ticked off his points. "First, suicides usually eat the gun. They'll open their mouth and shove it in. But, here, you can see how that bullet went right through her upper teeth. So, she had her mouth closed, her jaw clamped shut. She didn't do this to herself."

"And second?"

"Second would be the path of the bullet. Suicides turn the gun around. Not always, but often. They'll shove it in, turn it around and point it upward, so the muzzle is pressing against the hard palate. See?"

He feigned a gun with his hand and shoved his fingers into his mouth, dropping his jaw and arching his head back. His index and middle fingers tapped the top of his mouth, right behind his front teeth.

"So, the bullet would've gone upward," Blackie said. "It would've taken off the top of her head."

I had to close my eyes against *that* image.

"Here, let me show you something," Winslow said.

He gripped Brandy by the shoulder and rolled her onto her side, exposing a gaping wound in the nape of her neck. Then he pointed to a metallic object embedded in the wooden floorboards.

"The bullet entered through her mouth, then passed through the back of her throat. It even followed a slightly downward angle. I suspect she was on her knees, with the killer standing over her. I suspect that was the case with the both of them."

Blackie produced a penknife and worked the slug out with care. Blood, dust, and flesh stuck to it. He held it up to the light.

"I'd say it was a .32."

"Yup." Winslow eased Brandy back onto her back and nodded toward Andrew. "I'll have to open him up to get the bullet—there's no exit wound—but given the size of the entry wound, I'd say it's the same caliber."

The photographer called out that he was ready to start taking shots. Winslow gave a wave and said he was done. He and Blackie straightened up and the three of us walked a little ways away.

"I'll get the autopsy report to you within a day or two," Winslow said and headed out.

Blackie tapped me on the elbow and drew me to one side. I ended up with my back against the wall. He leaned an arm over my head and shoved the other in his pocket. He brought his face down close to mine and made his voice low and confidential.

"You know these people?" he said, his tone somewhere between a statement and a question.

"I've met Andrew socially, at dinner parties, but—"

"What about the wife?"

"Tessie? I've actually only met her once, and that was briefly. Why?"

"I want to know what kind of person she is. I want to know—"

"Whether she could've pulled the trigger?"

Silence. A cop's silence. I'd had my suspicions, but now I was certain as to why he'd had one of his cops call me to a crime scene in the middle of the night. It wasn't because he meant to do me any favors, to help me get a scoop.

"I don't know her that well."

He regarded me grimly. "Why would you try to protect her? You know I'm just going to find out the truth."

"That's exactly what I want you to do. Find the truth, and keep an open mind while doing it."

"An open mind? An open mind, you say? Now, why would you worry about that? Could it be because she confessed? Because she sat there, crying crocodile tears, and practically admitted to having done it? You mean, keep an open mind in the face of that?"

His mouth tightened and he gave me a hard stare.

"Did you find a weapon?" I asked.

"Not yet, but we will."

"Was anything taken?"

"You mean other than their lives?"

I didn't see a need to respond to that.

Having made his point, he dropped his arm and straightened up. "As you know, the killer didn't care about dough. As far as we can tell, the equipment's all here, but—"

He gestured for me to follow and led me deeper into the studio, to a room I hadn't realized was there. "It's the darkroom." He opened the door and stood aside.

The room had been trashed.

"Years of a man's work," he said. "Destroyed in minutes."

The damage was overwhelming. Every single photographic plate had been taken out and dashed to the floor, maybe even stomped on. It had taken a lot of energy to do that, a lot of determination, a lot of anger.

"C'mon," he said, tapping me on the shoulder. "There's more."

I followed him to an adjacent small room. Andrew's office. It held wooden shelves, a modest desk, and a chair. A cast-iron stove took up one corner. There was a sink, too. This room had probably served as a kitchen before Andrew turned it into an office. Papers were scattered everywhere; cameras, lenses, and books had been swept off the shelves and lay in heaps on the floor.

"That equipment," Blackie said. "It's expensive. It could've fetched a good price. But instead of stealing it, the killer destroyed it. And you know why? Because money wasn't the motive here. It was jealousy, revenge."

He turned away, not waiting for a response. I had to hurry to keep up as he strode past the death scene, where men were loading Andrew and Brandy onto stretchers.

The crowds parted as Blackie headed to the front entrance. There, he darted behind the counter. He had found Andrew's appointment book. It lay open, next to the cash register. He drew a thick index finger over the listings.

"He has dates for weddings, baptisms, First Holy Communions, Confirmations, and such. No jobs for tonight, but there is this." He tapped the page, then moved aside, making room for me.

I stepped up and read the notation, '7:15, BS.'

Brandy Sullivan.

He continued. "All the other appointments had the clients' names spelled out. It was only with Brandy here," he nodded toward the page, "that Andrew resorted to initials. He was hiding something and Tessie knew it. She knew it and she killed him for it—him and his little dancer friend."

His anger boiled over.

"That little show she put on back there? Don't believe it. She executed them. Pure and simple. She made them kneel, then shot them point-blank. Bam-bam. One right after the other."

I felt as though I'd been holding my breath ever since I'd stepped inside that studio, into this nightmare. Now, I felt like I was suffocating.

"I'm so sorry, baby. So, sorry," she'd said.

Images of Tessie sitting there, cradling Andrew's head, of his ruined eye and Brandy's damaged face, flashed before me. A lot of malice—a lot of rage—had powered those shots.

Yet, there she was, weeping. How had she gone from all that anger to *"So, sorry ...?"*

Not that it was impossible, but—

"I don't know, Blackie."

"What? You don't know what?"

I took a moment, trying to figure it out. "It doesn't make sense. There's the murder weapon. You didn't find one. If it's not here, then where is it?"

He shrugged. "She hid it."

"Are you saying she actually went out, hid the weapon, then came back?" I shook my head. "That doesn't sound right to me. If I killed someone, then I'd try to get away, and if I got away, I'd stay away. I sure wouldn't come back, sit here, weeping and basically telling the world that I did it."

"But that's you." He gave a dark smile. "You're smart and you can be calculating—and I mean that in the nicest way possible. You'd cover your tracks, and do it like a pro. But her?" He snorted. "She's not you, Lanie. Not by a long shot."

I thought of all the things I could say, should say, but before I could say anything, he held up a finger.

"There's one more thing." He lifted the book to reveal a large envelope that had been concealed beneath it. "This," he said, holding it up, "clarifies everything. It's proof positive that she did it."

I reached for the envelope, but he held it away, out of my reach.

"It's not the kind of thing a lady should see."

I was kind of touched to hear him say that. It wouldn't have occurred to many white men back then to call a colored woman a lady.

"Well, I do appreciate your kind attention to my sensibilities, but you needn't worry. Trust me, I've seen a lot, maybe even more than you. So, whatever it is, you might as well just give it here."

I held out my hand. He drew back and shook his head.

"Oh, come on," I said and snatched it out of his hand.

"Don't say I didn't warn you."

"You've just had me in to see a man shot through his eye and a woman shot through the mouth. Whatever this is, it can't be worse than that."

The envelope bore Brandy's name. So, whatever it contained was definitely meant for her. I felt Blackie's eyes on me as I opened it and drew out the contents.

Nude photos.

I kept my face expressionless.

Black and whites in which Brandy's skin glistened and glowed. In one photo, she lay draped over a punching bag, like a cat lounging on the bough of a tree; in another, she stood, embracing the erect bag, her head thrown back, her lips parted, one leg wrapped around it; in a third, she knelt before it, licking it. And so on.

I let the photos slide back into the envelope and handed it back to him.

"So, as far as Tessie's concerned, this closes it for you, right?"

He didn't answer. He didn't have to.

2

The next time I saw Tessie, it was at her arraignment, down at the Fifth District Prison, otherwise known as the Harlem Courthouse. She'd been found at the crime scene, asking her murdered husband for forgiveness. Her guilt was a given; the motive, obvious. The trial would be a mere formality, the legally-required preliminary to a ticket to Sing Sing and, most likely, an appointment with Old Sparky.

The four-story hall of justice was housed in a red brick building with a granite base. With its pinnacles and gables, its rounded arched windows and exterior clocks, the courthouse was an attractive building. But its outer beauty meant little to the souls who were judged inside its courtrooms or consigned to its dungeon-pit of a jail. The building wasn't even forty years old, but it reeked of fear and despair. The stench of cold sweat was already baked into its halls.

I hurried across the marble mosaic floors of the lobby and climbed the gilded staircase that spiraled upward to the main courtroom. My footsteps echoed across the hard surfaces, but the sound was lost in the general melee of the crowds present that day.

The courtroom itself flaunted soaring, vaulted ceilings, making it an elegant setting for the administration or misadministration of justice, as the case may be. Usually, it was impressive enough to create an atmosphere of nearly church-like awe among the visitors.

But not that day.

The courtroom was as noisy as a sports arena. It smelled of excitement and sweat. People pushed and shoved and tried to squeeze into places on packed benches. Reporters for the *Pittsburgh Courier*, the *Chicago Defender* and other colored newspapers had taken seats in the back. I slid in next to them. Had anyone managed to talk to Tessie? I asked.

"Nah," the reporter from the *Defender* said. "If you can believe the cops, they told Tessie she could talk to us, but she refused to."

"All of you? Wouldn't talk to none of you?"

"Nope." They all shook their heads.

If Tessie wouldn't talk to such influential papers as the *Courier* and *Defender*, then how likely was she to see me? After all, the *Harlem Chronicle*, though well-loved in Harlem, was, in a sense, still just a "small-town" paper, with only a local distribution and following.

Well, I decided, if I couldn't talk to her, then I'd talk to the visitors. Most of the crowd was just folks, people from the community. People in the rows ahead were elbowing each other, pointing toward the judge's bench.

"You just wait. Today, we gonna see some action," someone said.

I went to work, chatting them up, getting quotes for a story. I must've talked to at least five or six people. They pretty much said the same thing: that they adored Andrew and had never liked Tessie, never thought she was good enough for him.

"But this?" one said, "we never thought she'd ever do something like this."

"It ain't right," said another. "I'm telling you, it ain't right what she did, to shoot a man down like that. He was a good man, gave a lot to the community. And Brandy, she was something all right. There ain't never gonna be another one like her."

"Yeah," said a third. "It's a crying shame."

"And why are you here?" I asked. "What are you waiting for? Hoping to see?"

"We wants to send a message," said the first.

"A message?"

"Yeah," chimed in the second. "To let 'em know that this one—this one's different. They best not be letting her go."

"We know the police don't give a damn 'bout us," said the third. "They's always turning killers back out on the streets. But not this time. This time, they best be keeping this one in jail—for her own damn good."

There was a gaveling; the court was brought to order and people simmered down. I hurried back to my place with the reporters.

Everyone slid to the edge of their seats, waiting for Tessie's arrival. But another prisoner was brought in. A man charged with thievery, and after him came another. Then another, and another again. The court proceedings were short and to the point, so the prisoners were dealt with, one after the other, with decent efficiency. Even so, as the minutes crawled by, the proceedings became tedious and repetitive and the crowd got restless.

"I can't believe I actually took off work for this," someone grumbled.

Finally, after more than an hour, Tessie was brought in,

wearing shackles. The low grumbling stopped. There was a moment of silent gaping, then a swell of hisses and boos.

"Murderer!"

"Hussy!"

"We gonna show you! You gonna get yours!"

The judge banged his gavel again and again, demanding silence, and finally threatened to clear the courtroom. At that, the crowd simmered down, but the atmosphere remained openly hostile.

Led by the deputy, Tessie shuffled to her place at the defendant's table. She cut a small figure, reed-thin and dressed in drab jailhouse garb. Her eyes were red and swollen, her face puffy. Yet, she appeared calm, too calm after her demonstration of the night before. I wondered if she'd passed from acute grief into mind-numbed shock.

The charges were read. She didn't have a lawyer to speak for her, so she'd have to speak for herself. Would she be able to?

She was stronger, more resolute, than she appeared. She responded to the charges in a clear voice with a plea of not guilty. The judge set a date for a preliminary hearing, ten days hence, then pounded his gavel.

"Next!"

The whole thing took less than three minutes.

"That was it?" someone nearby whispered, expressing a sentiment reflected in the disappointment on many faces, and repeated in a murmuring of voices.

The court officer started to move Tessie out, but she resisted.

"A moment, please, your honor," she said.

The rustling in the courtroom ceased. Silence descended.

All eyes turned back to Tessie.

The judge raised a dark eyebrow. It was a slight gesture,

but it was enough to clearly express his judicial displeasure. "Your case has been dealt with. Now, move on."

The next prisoner was already lined up, waiting for entry.

"I know, and I'm sorry, your honor. I-I just wanted to ask about bail."

"Bail?" the judge repeated, his tone incredulous.

"Yes, sir. Could I have bail, please? I promise not to go anywhere. I'll stay here—"

"You most certainly will. You're charged with a capital crime. You're not going anywhere. Bail denied."

He pounded the gavel again and nodded for the officer to remove her.

Again, she resisted.

"I'm sorry, your Honor. Just one more thing."

"Ye-es?" His impatience turned the one syllable into two.

"I was wondering whether … when the time comes … whether I could at least get out to attend my husband's funeral."

A low murmur roiled the crowd.

"How dare she!"

"Why, that young heifer!"

"What nerve!"

The judge banged his gavel again and again, demanding silence. He leaned forward, glowering at Tessie.

"I repeat. You are *not* going *any*where. Except back to jail. And there you'll stay until the day of your hearing. Do you understand?"

A chastened Tessie nodded, her shoulders slumped.

"Now, leave my courtroom! Next!"

* * *

I followed the officer across the ground floor lobby, to a separate set of back stairs that led down, down, down into the bowels of the building. If the courtrooms upstairs were the inspiration of dreams, then the cells below were the stuff of nightmares.

The air was chilly and dank. The deeper we went, the darker it got, the more it stank of sour flesh, overrun toilets and sickly sweet disinfectant. I drew my coat closer, and burrowed my nose in its collar.

A heavy metal-plated door made of bars and set in a thick brick wall marked the arched entry to the passageways and the cells beyond. The warden selected a key from the large keyring dangling from his belt, opened the door and we crossed the threshold between freedom and detention.

Electrical wiring pipes scarred the ceiling overhead. They connected to a metal signal box above the doorway. Any trouble and an alarm would go off.

The jail consisted of five tiers, eight narrow cells on each tier, four to each side. The cells were built back-to-back. A month earlier someone had tried to dig his way out. He'd just found himself in another cell.

The cells themselves were walled in brick and fitted with two slender metal-frame bunk beds that were attached to the wall. Each cell also had a small washbasin and toilet bowl.

The officer allowed me into Tessie's cell to talk with her, and stood outside the bars, at a discreet distance where he could keep an eagle-eye on everything that went on.

Tessie and I sat on the lower bunk and exchanged brief pleasantries, taking each other's measure. Her calm demeanor still struck me as odd. On the one hand, her ability to get her emotions under control was admirable. On the other …

"So, how are you?" I asked.

"As well as can be expected." She gave a wan smile. "They brought in a doctor. He made me take something. It made me sleep. I can still feel it working."

That explained the outer calm. She said the jail staff was

being nice to her, which surprised her. She made small jests about the unexpectedness of life, which surprised me. She was neither known for, nor at first glance appeared to have, a sense of humor.

"Why did you agree to see me, when you wouldn't see the others?"

"I'm betting that your paper is read by more people here than the others are. And it's here that I'll be put on trial. It's from here they'll pick the jury."

How ironic, that my paper's "smallness" had for once worked in its favor.

"There's no guarantee that your jury will be from Harlem."

"I know. But it's a safe bet they won't be from Chicago or any one of those other places. Furthermore, I know you. I mean, I don't know you, but we've met before. And I know that Andrew thought highly of you. And so, I thought—oh, I don't know. I thought I might trust you. That you would be fair."

Her eyes searched mine, as mine had hers, trying to discern the truth.

"You will be, won't you? Be fair and tell it straight?"

I promised I would.

She looked down at her clasped hands. "I know why they arrested me. I understand that. And maybe I am partly to blame. Cause I did do wrong by him. I know that now. But I didn't kill him—or her. I never would've done that."

I wanted to believe her, but what she was saying didn't quite make sense. If she hadn't killed them, then why had she been sitting by his body, apologizing? What had she meant just now in saying she'd done *"wrong by him?"*

I was sorely tempted to ask but chose to pose a neutral question, instead. It was important to build trust and get better insight into her character. Furthermore, I wasn't there to judge her, just to gather news for a story. So, I would let her tell her story—*her fake story, her lie,* I could imagine Blackie saying—her own way.

Her story, as it was, was simple. Her voice thickened as she told it. At times, she blinked to keep back tears. But mostly, she stayed steady.

She stated that the evening before, Andrew said he'd be working late.

"I was all right with that. It didn't happen often, but when it did I had nothing against it. But then, it got late and he wasn't back, so I got worried and decided to go on down to the studio."

The shop windows were dark and he'd put up the sign saying he was closed.

"That didn't mean anything. He often did that when he was in the darkroom and didn't want to be disturbed."

She knocked, politely at first. When that didn't get a response, she rapped harder. Finally, in frustration, she grabbed the door handle and gave it a twist.

To her surprise, the door popped open.

"Andrew always locked it, when he worked late. He never would've left it open like that."

Inside, she turned on the lights. The glass display cases containing picture frames, white plaster statues of Mary and Jesus and other knickknacks: they were all fine. Everything looked all right, but something felt wrong.

Where was Andrew?

She walked to the large rear room that served as the studio, turned on the light, and stood there wondering what two long bags of laundry were doing on the floor.

It didn't surprise me that she mistook two corpses for laundry. I'd heard stranger tales of what can happen when the mind refuses to accept what the eyes can see.

Tessie said she remembered little after that. One minute

she was standing over her dead husband and the next she was sitting in a jail cell.

"They tell me I was asking him for forgiveness."

"You were." I watched her closely. "Was it for having killed him?"

"No. I never would've hurt him." Her eyes were large behind the bottle-glass lenses. "I would've killed myself first, before I ..."

"Then what were you asking forgiveness for?"

She averted her gaze.

"Tessie," I said, my tone gentle, "you said you did him wrong. What did you mean by that?"

She pressed her lips together and shook her head. Tears slid down her cheeks, and she rapidly wiped them away with the heel of her hand.

I took out a hanky, held it up and opened so the guard could see I wasn't concealing anything in it, and handed to her.

"Was Andrew stepping out with Brandy Sullivan?"

Her eyes briefly shocked open wide. Then, she denied it with a shake of her head and dabbed at her eyes.

"Did he say he was going to meet her last night?"

She stared down at her hands, working the handkerchief into a tight ball.

I let the silence ride, hoping she'd feel compelled to fill it. When that didn't work, I filled it myself—with some harsh facts.

I told her how the police had found Andrew's appointment book and that they'd found the photos. I didn't mince words, but I didn't embellish them, either. There was no need to. She listened, evidently stricken. When I was done, she asked me about the pictures, in detail, and I answered her, in truth.

"You knew about the two of them, didn't you?"

She was quiet, withdrawing into herself. For a moment, I thought I'd lost her. But then, she put a hand to her mouth and choked back a sob.

"Andrew was faithful," she whispered, tears slipping down her cheeks. "He didn't cheat on me. I know he didn't. He wasn't like that."

Did she honestly believe that? Or was she just trying to sound as though she did?

"All right. Fine. If you didn't shoot them, then who do you think did?"

That was one question she answered but quick.

"Big Earl," she sniffed and swiped at her cheeks. "He did it. He hated Andrew. If he thought Andrew was …"

"Was what?"

She clamped her mouth shut and shook her head. I waited. She closed her eyes and drew a deep breath. When she spoke, it was with a tone of profound weariness and regret.

"I know it looks bad. But please believe me. I loved my man. I loved him and I did not shoot him. If you want to find the real killer, then take a look at that woman's husband, Big Earl."

Her tone hardened, growing heated as anger replaced regret.

"He did it. I'm telling you, it was him. That prizefighter. Big Earl. He's the one."

3

Human nature can be disappointingly predictable, but it's often surprising, too. Take the favor Tessie asked of me: I didn't see it coming. I thought it odd, not because it was odd in and of itself, but because it didn't fit her public persona.

I agreed to do it—it was well within my abilities and I saw no reason not to—but I found myself wondering whether she was playing me, wondering once more as to the truth of her motive and who was the real Tessie King.

Andrew and Tessie had shared an apartment with his mother in a five-story apartment building on Hamilton Place in West Harlem. Entering the lobby, I saw that it had once been beautiful, but now spoke of neglected grandeur. It was wide and spacious, with tiled floors, potted palms, mirrored walls, and molded ceilings, but the palms were dry; the mirror chipped and the once white tiles a mottled gray.

Like many turn-of-the-century buildings in Harlem, this one had been designed for the wealthy and the white. Now, that the place was occupied by the poor and the colored, the owners were letting it go to seed.

As I climbed the stairs, holding the bouquet of roses I'd picked up along the way, I caught a whiff of collard greens, ham hocks and sweet potatoes. Many of the tenants in these buildings were refugees from the Angry South. That's what Hamp used to call it. The Angry South. That place where colored men, women, and children could be lynched or burned alive just for looking at a white person 'wrong.' That included colored soldiers who had survived the Great War on foreign soil, only to be murdered by their fellow Americans back home.

Driven by fear as much as by hope, wave upon wave of the folk were heading north. Most went to my hometown, Chicago, but a lot set their sights on Harlem, especially the ones who had dreams of finding good jobs and living prejudice-free.

In New York, those dreams collided with the harsh reality of low-paying jobs and high-priced apartments, in buildings full of vermin, lacking in heat and hot water, packed with people infected with tuberculosis or sick with pneumonia.

But it didn't matter. None of it mattered.

Because, grim as it could be, the reality of Harlem was still better than the nightmare of what had been left behind. The dream endured because it still offered hope. It still offered refuge from the terror of the burning cross and the lynch mob's noose.

I thought about all this as I climbed those stairs and reached the second-floor landing. I thought of it as I saw the apartment doors lining the long hallway.

Each door represents a story, a tale of survival, of hope ...

My gaze came to rest on the door that footed the end of the corridor.

and sometimes ... of tragedy.

I knocked and waited. Several seconds went by. There was no answer, so I knocked again. When there was still no answer, I started to move away. Maybe, I could find a neighbor to talk to. But then I heard a rustling sound behind the door and a thin, querulous voice called out.

"Who is it?"

Moving back to the door, I answered. "My name's Lanie, Lanie Price."

There came the sound of a lock being undone and the door opened up a crack. A thin elderly woman stood behind it. Mamie King. Andrew's mother. The resemblance was evident.

Even in grief, she was elegant. Her black dress was simple but stylish, and her silver-white hair was done in perfect finger waves. Her knotted fingers gripped a white lace handkerchief and her dark eyes were reddened. She gazed at me quizzically.

"Yes?"

I had never met Andrew's mother, but I'd heard him speak of her. I knew that he loved her, that he believed that he and his mother and Tessie all got along very well. She would be an important person to talk to, but I believe in letting families grieve in peace, so I wouldn't have approached her if it hadn't been for Tessie. It was at Tessie's bidding that I was there. It was Tessie who'd said, *"Would you please look in on her for me?"*

I had wondered whether the request was meant to create sympathy. Then I decided it didn't matter. Visiting Andrew's mother was a kindness that needed doing. I had no intentions of "interviewing" Mrs. King, but if she made statements that proved interesting, I fully intended to pursue them. As for Tessie's motives, she must've known that having me talk to Mrs. King carried certain risks and could backfire.

I explained that I was a reporter, "for the *Chronicle*."

"Oh, now that you say that, I know you by your picture.

You're the young lady who writes that society column. I enjoy it."

"Thank you."

"You're here about my son."

"Yes, but I could come back later if—"

"No, it's all right. Better to get this over with. To tell you the truth, I'm surprised that more of you newspaper people ain't been here yet. But I s'pose that'll change soon. Come in."

Who had given her the news? Had she had to spend the night alone with it?

The front door opened onto a long narrow hallway, with rooms branching off on either side. The hardwood floors gleamed from good regular polishings and the open doors showed rooms that were as neat as a pin. The building may have been going to seed, but this apartment wasn't. It was clean and well-kept and smelled lightly of rosewater.

She led me down the hall to the front room, where she offered coffee; I declined.

"Thank you, but no thank you, Mrs. King."

"Call me Mama, Mama King. Everybody does."

She accepted the flowers graciously and went off to find a vase and put them in water, leaving me alone.

The room had high ceilings and tall windows with good views of the sky. On sunny days, the room must've been bright and cheerful. But it was cold and gray that day, and the light was subdued and mournful.

A plump beige sofa sat to one side, with matching night tables and a round coffee table of dark wood. Crocheted lace doilies covered every flat surface. A breakfront displayed fine silver and chinaware. The walls held tiers of photographs depicting family life: beach parties, picnics, and car outings. This had been a happy home, comfortable and content.

The soft glow of a lamp drew me to a narrow side table. It was like a shrine. The light gently illuminated a portrait of

Andrew in military uniform, wearing the insignia of a corporal and a badge bearing the sign of a coiled rattler. It was the sign of the *Black Rattlers*, also known as the Fighting 369th, also known as the Harlem Hell Fighters.

The 369th was the first colored regiment to reach the battlefields of War War I France and the first of the Allied troops to achieve the banks of the Rhine in Germany, serving under French command. By the end of the war, the regiment had endured months and months in combat, among the longest of any American regiment.

Two military medals were on display next to the portrait. I bent to get a closer look and saw that they were each a *Croix de Guerre*. The French government had formally acknowledged the courage of our colored troops in the war. It had awarded the entire 369th for its bravery. In addition, the French had honored some soldiers with individual medals and the Legion of Honor.

So, Andrew had not only been a talented photographer but a war hero, too. I would use that, write about it, make sure to include it in my piece.

"You know, that's how he got started in photography," said a voice next to me.

Startled, I turned to find Mama King at my side. She had returned with the flowers in a vase and now leaned down to make space for it on the little shrine.

"He found a camera on a dead German soldier and started taking pictures of everything he could, the good and the bad, and he wrote little stories to go with them. Of course, he didn't just sit back and watch. He fought, too. Fought bravely."

"Yes, I see he got an individual medal. Is that right?"

"Saved his men from a bunch of German soldiers. Killed one of them—a captain, I think—and managed to pull one of the other American soldiers to safety. The man had gotten shot in the leg and couldn't move, but my Andrew was there to rescue him."

She went quiet for several seconds. "He was over there for eighteen months. After that, he wasn't the same. He used to tell me how he'd have to go in after the fighting, to search for survivors and bury the dead. Hundreds of dead. Some of them literally cut in half, blown to bits. My son saw things he could never forget, things no man should ever have to see."

Her words reminded me of what Hamp had told me about his experiences as a medic in the war. He, too, had seen things he could barely speak of.

She was studying me. "Do you promise to write nothing that would hurt my son? I think he's suffered enough. Don't you?"

Privately, I thought to myself that Andrew was finally beyond hurting, but this little old woman wasn't.

"Don't worry. The last thing I want to do is bring you more pain."

Despite her restraint, or perhaps because of it, her grief was palpable. It struck me that the photographs on the walls showed only her and Andrew and Tessie. Andrew might've been not only her only son but her only child. With him gone, she had no one.

"You know, I remember Andrew talking about you," she said, "you and your husband."

She took a seat on the sofa and patted the space next to her for me to join her.

"He liked you," she said. "Told me he was going to invite you two to dinner."

Going to. How they echoed, those two words! Such simple words. We say them all the time. *Going to.* They casually assume a future, one that in this case would never be.

"This time yesterday," she said, "he was here. He was still *alive.* And now ... he's gone. How can that be? How can a person be here one minute, then gone the next? And all those hopes and dreams and plans …? Gone—in an instant! How can that be?"

She furrowed her brow. "For it all to be taken away—just like that. And why? Why would anyone do that?"

She swallowed hard. "When they came to tell me, they was very thoughtful. They took me down to the mortuary, the one down on 29th Street and Avenue A. They said I had to identify him."

Her breath caught and she put a hand to her chest, obviously finding it hard to breathe. "My God, why do that to him? Shoot him in the eye, like that? Like they was making a mockery of him being a photographer."

"I'm so sorry you had to see that."

"Police said, they was going to autopsy him tomorrow— him and that dancer, Brandy. Said they got to cut him open, to get out the bullet."

Tears brimmed in her eyes. "He was a good man. Good, solid, kind—and hard-working. He didn't … he didn't deserve this."

"No, he didn't."

She looked at me with a sudden thought. "Have you talked to Tessie?"

"I just came from seeing her."

"What did she look like?"

"About the way you'd expect."

She nodded, pensive. "She loved my son. Adored him, in fact. And she was good for him. But …"

"But what?"

She didn't answer. She seemed lost in a welter of pain.

"You know … it's just becoming real," she said. "Before, it wasn't real. I couldn't accept it. And I'm not sure I can now. But I'm getting there. I guess I'm getting there."

"It'll take time," I told her, thinking about my grief over

Hamp. I sought words to comfort her but found none. There are none. All I could say was, "It'll take time."

"I know." She reached out to me, put her hand over mine. "I heard about your husband. I'm very sorry that happened. He was a good man, too."

"Yes, he was."

She sighed. "Good men die young these days."

"Yes, ma'am. They sometimes do."

4

The kettle whistled and Mama King asked me to help her in the kitchen. She insisted upon taking out her best silver tea service, with cream and sugar, and little sugar cookies. I carried the tray back into the parlor, where we sat on her sofa and she resumed where we'd left off.

"You want to know about Tessie," she said. "I know that's why you're here. You want to know about her, as much as you do about my son."

"Yes, but the fact is, I wouldn't be here if it weren't for her. I wouldn't have dared disturb you. But she asked me to come by and check on you."

"Did she now?" Thoughtful, Mama King took a sip of her tea. "Tessie has a lot of good qualities. She's smart and she knows it. But she's not so confident about ... well, about the rest. She just couldn't never believe that my son loved her the way she loved him. And in the end, I got to wonder, whether it was jealousy, the jealousy, that got her."

She was only echoing what Blackie had said but coming from her, the words carried weight. It hurt to hear them and I was surprised to find myself wanting to defend Tessie, to say, *Of course, she was insecure. When the world keeps telling you you're not good enough for your man, you're bound to start wondering.*

"Did they fight?"

She paused. "Sometimes."

"Like last night?" It was a shot in the dark.

Mama King drew a deep breath and gave a grim nod. "Like last night. Tessie ... she got herself all worked up. So worked up. Said he was messing with that dancing girl. It wasn't true, mind you, and he told her so. He told her she was wrong, all kinds of wrong, and that he'd never stepped out on her, but that nobody would've blamed him if he had. He said that if she didn't change, he'd walk out that door and never look back.

"Of course, he didn't mean it," she quickly added. "He never would've left her—or me."

"But did Tessie know that?"

"She should've."

She paused, then asked me: "I don't suppose Tessie told you any of this?"

"No."

"Of course, not."

But she must've known, I thought, *that you would tell me.* "This disagreement, what time did it happen?"

"About six."

"You were here the whole time?"

"In my room." She gestured toward the back. "I closed my door, but I could still hear them."

I hesitated. "Mama King, I mean no disrespect, but you do know that Andrew and Brandy were found together. Doesn't that indicate that—"

"No," she said firmly. "There's no way my son woulda been messing with that woman. She was just another customer to him. That was it. That was as far as it went.

Andrew liked theater people. They made for good business. They liked to have their pictures taken. They knew how to pose before a camera and they always came back for more.

"For better or worse, he loved Tessie. He may have said he would've left her—in the heat of anger he might've said that—but he wouldn't have done it. And yes, I do think Tessie knew that."

But had she? Had Tessie realized that Andrew's threat was empty? Or had she gone to the studio, gripped with the fear that she'd gone too far, then seen him there with Brandy and lost her mind?

I could see it all so clearly, the images running through my head like a moving picture show. There she was, setting out, scared and hurt and practicing how she was going to apologize and get him to stay, but then finding him with Brandy and getting all angry and it going all wrong. I could see the gun in her hand and—

Wait a minute. My thoughts skidded to a halt. *The gun, again. Where did it come from? Was it there at the studio, available for her to grab? Or did she bring it with her?*

"Mama King, did Tessie or Andrew keep a gun?"

"Well, *he* did. He had to. You know what it's like out there. He was always worried about someone trying to rob him."

She wasn't sure whether the gun had been at the house or at the studio the night before, she said, but she did know the make and caliber. "A .32 automatic."

The same make and caliber Doc Winslow said had been used in the murders and Tessie would've had easy access to it.

5

"Mama King, do you think she did it?"

I probably shouldn't have asked, but the words slipped out before I realized it.

"No," she said, surprising me.

"No?"

She shook her head. "I know what folks are saying, but I know her. I know that girl. Oh, she's a little strange all right. Can come off kind of arrogant. But she's got a good heart. She's not selfish. And she knows right from wrong."

Not selfish.

Murderers are nothing if not selfish. Yet here was the victim's mother saying that the woman accused of having killed her son lacked that essential quality for murder.

"Mama King, who gave you the news? Was it Detective Blackie?"

She thought for a moment, wrinkling her forehead. "I'm sorry, I don't remember his name. I do remember he had an accent. Irish, I think."

"Did you tell him about the argument?"

"I was in such shock. I don't know. I can barely

remember."

Her gaze returned to the photo on the side table. A sad smile graced her lips. "He was my only child, you know? I was proud of him. Naturally, I was. And when he brought Tessie home, I was a little ... Well, to be honest, I was a little unsure. But then I got to know her. And I knew he'd picked right." Her chin trembled. "Do you think, if I went down there, they'd let me in to see her?"

"I don't see why they wouldn't." I reached out and gave her hands a squeeze.

She dabbed her eyes with her handkerchief. "You know, I'd hoped for grandchildren. Now ... there's nothing, nothing but this big place. Seven big empty rooms. Nothing but loss."

"You've got other family? Someone to come and be with you?"

"My neighbor, she come over soon as she heard the news, but you know how it is. Folks come round the first few days. Some of 'em just cause they nosey. Those ones don't stay long, thank God. But after a while, even the ones who care, they go 'way, too. No, I ain't got nobody now. No one, but Tessie."

She gave a bitter chuckle. "Ain't that something? I ain't got nobody but the woman they say killed my son."

Tears seeped from her eyes. "Maybe, she did do it and I just don't want to admit it. Cause maybe I'm just a sad, stupid old woman who's scared to be alone. You asked me if I think she did it. I said I didn't. But the fact is, I don't know. I just don't know. All I know is that my boy is gone. He's gone and he ain't never coming back."

This proud, dignified woman broke down and wept. I took her in my arms, held her shaking shoulders and wondered how I could help her.

Slowly, the sobs eased. Mama King straightened up and dabbed at her damp face. "I'm sorry," she whispered.

"You have nothing to apologize for." I refilled her teacup and handed it to her. "So, tell me, if it wasn't Tessie, then who do you think might've done it?"

"It was that man. That big old boxing man."

"Brandy's husband?"

She nodded. It seems like he was the suspect of the day.

That is, if you didn't count Tessie.

Just then the bell rang.

"Are you expecting anyone?" I asked, worried about it being another reporter.

She shook her head. "Would you mind answering? Just, no reporters, please. You were okay. But not nobody else. Not one of them. Not today."

I promised to beat them away with a broomstick if I had to and headed down the hall to the door. The irony and potential hypocrisy of the situation did not escape me. Here I was, telling other reporters to stay away. I was sure that wouldn't go over too well.

Never mind.

The fact was, Mama King did not deserve or need to be hounded by my colleagues at this time, or at any time for that matter. While I was there, I would see that she wasn't. I was fairly sure that most people didn't even know that Andrew had a mother living in Hamilton Heights, but I was also sure they'd soon find out.

Briefly, I thought about moving her, at least temporarily, into my townhouse. But then I realized that the last thing she needed was to be uprooted from her home. This apartment was not only a reminder of her losses but of her blessings. In the end, it could give her solace and strength. Furthermore, here she had neighbors to care for her.

Indeed, I hoped she did.

As a matter-of-fact, it turned out to be one of those neighbors—well, not a neighbor exactly. The visitor was a church lady: short and stout, wrapped snugly in a sleek black Persian lamb coat. The face was only vaguely familiar, but the name, Coriander Dill, was instantly recognizable. I had seen it on a lot of society club memberships. She recognized me right away and explained that she attended the same church as Mama King. When I led her into the living room, the joy and relief on Mama King's face were unmistakable.

It turned out that Mrs. Dill and her ladies circle had arranged a full suite of care for Mama King—and, before I could get the words out, she was explaining to me in a gentle voice that as much as she appreciated my work as a journalist, she was not about to let a single one of my colleagues come within a mile of Mama King.

"You tell them that for me, OK?"

I gave her my word that I would do what I could. Then I turned to Mama King to say my good-byes.

She took me by the hand—her grip was strong—and pulled me toward her. I had to bend down to meet her gaze.

"Promise me something," she said.

"Yes?"

"Promise me, you'll do what you can to make sure Tessie's not railroaded into prison for something she didn't do."

I hesitated. "Mama King, I'm not a cop or a lawyer. I—"

"I know who you are. You are Lanie Price, and you know how to do things. I've read about you, the things you've done, the truths you've found that others have missed."

"I will try, but suppose—just suppose—Tessie's guilty. Then—"

"Then she's guilty. And I'll know that she's getting what she deserves. All I'm asking for is the truth. That's all I want."

I understood. Despite her words, Mama King wanted Tessie to be innocent. She wanted me to help prove that innocence. I promised her I'd do what I could, but privately, I doubted it would be enough.

* * *

I told Mama King I'd stop by again to see her. Then I set out to knock on doors. Someone was home in just about every apartment: shift workers, mostly. Some of them came to the door, rubbing their eyes, having just fallen asleep. Some were grumpy, but none were rude—especially when they learned who I was and why I was there. They invited me in.

People often ask me how I get people to talk. It's not that hard. I suspect that folks often hope I'll tell them more than they plan to tell me. But the fact is, the one thing a lot of people like more than hearing gossip is telling it themselves. That right there takes care of a good chunk of the people. Then, there are the ones who are simply lonely and happy to have anyone stop by. So, it was easy to get the neighbors to talk that day. If anything, it was hard to get them to stop.

I managed to talk to nine sets of residents, some on the same floor as the Kings, some who lived above and some who lived below them, before I decided I'd had enough. All reported hearing the same thing: Tessie's accusations, Andrew's denials, then Tessie's weeping. The couple often argued, they said, but they'd had an especially loud argument the night before.

I now knew what Tessie had refused to admit, that she'd not only fought with Andrew but had done so in a jealous fit, one that provided more than enough motive for murder.

The neighbors also let me know something else.

Turns out I wasn't the first person to have come around asking. Blackie and his men had been there before me. While I was talking to Tessie down at the courthouse, they'd been up here, canvassing the building. I'd missed them by no more than thirty minutes. The people I talked to had all seen Blackie. Some said they'd chosen to share nothing; others, however, had shared aplenty.

6

Big Earl. He was an obvious alternative suspect and I was definitely interested in talking to him, but first I had another stop to make. I headed down to West 135th Street and the station house.

The unheated station house was chilly and smelled of old greasy food, the result of officers eating at their desks.

The gray-haired sergeant at the front desk was named Wilkins. I'd seen him in passing for years, but in all my comings and goings to the station house we'd never exchanged more than the necessary words with one another. He had never been disrespectful. I just knew him to be a stern old-timer, and I wasn't sure he approved of Blackie's friendship with a reporter, and a female colored one at that. He waved me through.

Blackie was at his desk, munching a jelly donut, his shirt sleeves rolled up. Briefly, I wondered at his tolerance for the cold. He looked delighted to see me.

"Got a minute?" I asked.

"Be my guest." He gestured to the chair next to his desk.

Now, Blackie isn't rude or inhospitable, but he isn't

normally all that jovial, either, especially when it comes to seeing me. For some reason, he associates me with trouble. Lately, he's even taken to accusing me of "always throwing a wrench in the works." So, it was a bit unsettling to have him so friendly and all. Something was up.

"It's about Big Earl," I said.

"What about him?"

"Have you looked at him?"

"Nope." He took another bite.

"Why not?"

"Well, unlike Tessie—who I'll remind you has just about confessed to the murders—Big Earl's got the perfect alibi."

"Which is?"

"At the time of the killing, he was in the ring. Scores of people saw him go ten rounds at J.B.'s Gym. Scores more saw him hanging out at Small's Paradise afterward."

"Big Earl's got scratch, right?"

"Some."

"Then, how can the man have a 'perfect' alibi? He can afford to hire hoods to do his killing for him."

He shrugged. "Well, we'll find out soon enough, won't we?"

"What does that mean?"

"We found the gun."

No wonder he was looking so pleased with himself.

"Where?"

"About half a block away. In a trashcan."

"That doesn't prove that she put it there."

"I figured you'd say something like that. Sometimes, I think contradicting me is second nature to you."

The words were a mite harsh, but he said them with a smile to soften their sting. He could afford to be kind, even a bit patronizing. After all, he was sure he was in the right and, to be fair, he might be.

"Well, I will agree that finding the gun is a good development," I said. "It can only bring us closer to the truth."

"Aye. That it will."

"You're sure it's the one used in the killings?"

"Caliber matches. It's a Ruby M1915, a .32 automatic, a French sidearm—"

"French?"

"The Frenchies used them in the trenches during the war. Holds nine shots instead of the usual six or seven. Very easy to use, even for someone who isn't used to guns."

"But what would Tessie be doing with a French sidearm?"

"It was probably Andrew's. He fought during the war, didn't he? And under French command. We're checking for prints. I'll bet you two-to-one, we'll find hers. You'll see."

I'd never seen him so smug.

He finished his donut, then wiped his mouth. "Lanie, this would be a first."

"For what?"

"First time I've ever heard you say something you don't mean."

"As to what?"

"The gun. You're not happy we found it."

"I didn't say I was. I said it's good you've found it, and I do believe that. I just ..." I shrugged.

"What?"

I hesitated. Blackie was one of my favorite people. He was a good cop, but he was a cop, and an Irish one at that— surely, one of the most stubborn breed of men the Good Lord made. Blackie had already made up his mind as to Tessie's guilt and he wasn't going to change it. Not easily. Not when he thought he had the case all sewn up. And he didn't care all that much about loose threads. The last thing he wanted was to hear me say, 'But it doesn't make sense.'

I said it, anyway.

"It doesn't make sense."

"Ah, Lanie," he balled up his napkin and threw it down with a sigh. "You're just trying to throw a wrench in the works. I knew you would. You always do. But this time—" He wagged a finger at me. "This time, it won't work. We've got the gun, we've got motive, and for all intents and purposes, we've got a confession."

"But …"

"But what?"

He waited, but I didn't continue. "Lanie?"

I shook my head. "Nope. You don't want to hear." I took hold of my purse and stood to go. "I'll just leave."

"Lanie, please."

I raised an eyebrow but said nothing. We engaged in another one of those useless staring contests he always lost. He became more and more tightlipped. Finally, he burst out with it.

"OK, fine. I'll listen. Sit down and tell me. What about this is bothering you?"

"All right, then." I sat back down and perched on the edge of the seat. "It's the same thing as before."

"And that was …?"

"Why would she shoot them, go a block away and hide the gun, then go back and sit there, holding him, weeping and waiting for the cops to find her? You don't hide the evidence, then go back and confess. You get away, you stay away."

"Look, she was there—right there," he thumped his desk for emphasis. "She was begging him for forgiveness. That tells me she did it. *She* killed him. Are you honestly telling me you think she didn't?"

"I think there's room for doubt, yes." I searched for words to explain. "I admit it. When I saw Tessie there and heard her pleas for forgiveness, at first, at that moment, I thought she'd probably killed him, too. It didn't fully make sense, but … there it was."

"And so what's changed?"

"The more I think about it, the more I think there are too many details, discrepancies, that need explaining."

"Like what?"

"Like, who called the police? Was it Tessie?"

"Her?" He gave a disgusted grunt. "She wouldn't have had the decency—or the guts. It was a passerby did it. Said there'd been a killing and that he'd heard her screaming."

"What else did he say?"

"What d'you mean, what else? Nothing else."

"You didn't interview him?"

"No. Why would I? No!"

"Are you going to?"

"No—how? We don't even know who he is."

"He didn't give his name?"

"Lanie."

"I'm just asking."

He made a visible effort to be patient. "As you should know, it's not that unusual for people not to give their names. They get nervous."

"I know, but—"

"But what?"

There was no mistaking the edge to his voice.

"Nothing," I said, working hard to keep the edge from mine.

"Lanie?"

"Yes?" I said, getting up to go.

"You wouldn't be thinking of going to see Big Earl, would you?"

I paused. "What if I was?"

"I'd say stay away from him."

"As in today, tomorrow, or forever?"

He didn't like that. I should've cared, but I didn't.

"Big Earl's got a manager," Blackie said. "He goes by the name of Teddy Banks, and he's been known to fix a fight or two."

"Mob-connected?"

"Of course, he is. Boxing and the mob—they go hand in glove. So, keep away from them. You hear me? They're dangerous. And they don't take kindly to strangers."

"Don't worry. I'll be careful. But who'll they see when they look at me? Just a little reporter. That's all. A woman and a colored one at that. They won't take me seriously."

7

B ack at the newsroom, I stopped by to see my boss, Sam Delaney. Sam was not only our editor but our primary sports writer. He was a walking archive of sports history, from the trivial to the significant. I had no abiding interest in sports, but I loved to read his copy. His stories were written with passion and wit. He kept his office neat and clean.

Organized. A perfect reflection of his mind.

Sam was pounding the keys when I walked in, sleeves rolled up, his broad shoulders stretching the material of his white shirt. He looked up and greeted me with a serious expression. "Let me guess. You want to talk about Big Earl?"

"Am I that obvious?" I plopped down in the chair next to his desk.

He pounded out another line, squinted at it and made a correction, then rolled the sheet out of the typewriter, put it on his desk, and swiveled round to face me.

"So, talk to me," he said, giving me his full attention.

I had already spoken to him that morning before going down to the courthouse and filled him in on what had gone down at the crime scene. I now told him about my meeting with Tessie and Mama King. He agreed that in addition to the main story on the investigation into the King-Sullivan murders, I should do a profile piece on each of the victims and their families.

"That includes Big Earl," I said. "I'm hoping you can give me some background on him."

Now, I already knew something about Big Earl. Everyone did. He was a celebrity among the colored folk in Harlem. To give him his due, he was known among the whites, too, cheered on by the many who loved the fights or liked to party in Harlem. But what I knew was generalities; I was hoping for specifics.

"Big Earl started out in Georgia," Sam said. "He hit the circuit and arrived in Harlem two years ago. He's strong and he's fast. He could've been another Joe Gans, but lately, he's been looking more and more like a has-been. He hangs out at J.B.'s Gym, over on 127th and Lenox. They say he's working out hard, but his days of pulling in the purses appear to be over."

"He's already reached his peak?"

"Yup. "

"But the man's not even thirty."

Sam started in on the stats detailing Big Earl's wins and losses. Very informative to others, I'm sure, but meaningless to me. My eyes began to glaze over. Then Sam said something that snapped me right back to attention.

"Of course, the harder things get for him, the meaner he gets. He was always paranoid, always jealous, and he beats his women."

"Did he beat Brandy?"

"I don't know, but I do know that he beat the women before her. I saw the results."

"The cops are thinking jealousy was the motive. If that's the case, then Big Earl had just as good a motive as Tessie."

"But she confessed. She was found with the body and she said she did it."

"It's not as clear-cut as all that."

Sam gave me a skeptical eye.

"I mean, it was," I admitted, "but it wasn't. Not really."

"Playing detective again?"

"No," I said firmly. "I never have and never will 'play' detective. I just ask questions, a few good questions."

He raised an eyebrow and gave me the look, *that* look. "Sorry, Lanie. You can't kid a kidder. You want to rope Big Earl into what happened to his wife last night."

"Are you a fan, trying to protect him?"

"Heck, no! I just think—"

"He *is* roped into it, as you put it, just by being the spouse. The spouse is always the most likely suspect."

"Yes, and the cops have a spouse, in custody. But," he held up a hand to stave off my rebuttal, "if that's the angle you're going for—that jealousy's the thing and that Big Earl could've done it—"

"Is *just as likely* to have done it—"

"If that's what you intend to show, then you're going to have a hard time doing it."

"I can imagine."

"*Can* you?"

I narrowed my eyes. "Clearly, you have something specific in mind."

"What do you know about Big Earl's manager, Teddy Banks?"

I shrugged. "Blackie said something about him."

"Banks is on a first-name basis with movers and shakers from Harlem Heights to Tammany Hall. He mainly runs with Owney Madden, though."

"That gangster who bought the Cotton Club?"

"Yeah. Madden's also in the fights racket."

"He backs colored fighters?"

"No. He *uses* them to make his fighters look good. It's an open secret that Madden manages many of the top boxers." He counted off on his fingers: "Primo Carnera, Maxie Rosenbloom, Jimmy Braddock. Madden's been into boxing and bootlegging for more than a couple of years now and the Cotton Club's given him a perfect front for it. Not that he hides it that much. He does it right out in the open. Even sells beer in there, bottles of it, with his name on it. Madden's a convicted killer and he controls Banks. He's the one calling the shots, not Banks."

"I still don't get it. Why would Banks, who's managing a colored boxer, throw in with Madden, if all Madden does is try to get colored boxers to fail?"

"Think about it."

I shrugged. "No idea."

"Every time a boxer wins, he gets a boost in value. He gets access to bigger fights and bigger purses."

"Okay ..."

"Boxing is big money, Lanie. Revenues for this past quarter were more than a couple of million."

"That much?"

"You get the right fighter in there, you can sell out Madison Square Garden, pull in a million-dollar gate. And a well-done fix? It could be worth tens of thousands, maybe even hundreds."

I tapped the edges of the armrest. "So, if Big Earl has blood on his hands, then it's a sure bet that Banks is moving to cover him."

"They're mean people, Lanie. You don't want to mess with them."

I nodded. "Thanks for the warning." I stood and started to go. At the door, I paused and said over my shoulder, "Hmm-hmph. That cologne? It sure smells good."

8

J.B.'s was one of those what-you-see-is-what-you-get kind of places, and what you saw wasn't much. But from the smell of it, it drew dedicated fighters, committed to the core.

The place was weathered and scruffy, pungent with the rancid odors of stale sweat, dirty socks and cheap cologne. It was a small but open space, its brick walls plastered with newspaper clippings and autographed photos of past and present champions. The steady rhythmic thumping of fighters hitting punching bags filled the air.

More than a few eyes turned my way, their owners' surprise evident at seeing a woman penetrate this all-male space.

A gentleman with a frayed cap walked up to me. "Can I help you, miss?"

"No, but thank you," I said, looking past him. I had spotted Big Earl, sitting next to one of the rings. "I see who I'm here for."

He glanced over his shoulder and saw who I meant. "I'm sorry, I can't let you bother him. He's—"

Too late. I was already walking past him, headed for my target.

Eyes followed me with stares that ranged from curious to suspicious to outright hostile. But nobody made a move or said a thing. Maybe, they were too shocked to.

Big Earl must've just finished a training round. He was a huge man, perched on a tiny bench, unwrapping gloves the size of large coconuts.

Sitting next to him, whispering in his ear, was a little pale-skinned guy: Teddy Banks, I assumed. He was dapper in a silver-gray suit with a black shirt and ice white tie. He had a blunt, bullet-shaped nose, thin red lips and the flat dead eyes of a shark.

Banks broke off when I strode up. Both men stood. Big Earl's face was puffy. Was it from grief, too many punches, or too much drink?

I introduced myself and expressed my condolences.

"Brandy was a good woman," he told me.

"I just came from talking to Tessie King. She says she didn't do it."

"Yeah? What else would she say?"

"What about you?"

"What about me?"

"Are you actually asking my client whether he killed his wife?" Banks asked.

"The thing is, I heard that when the police asked your client what he was doing when the killings went down, he said he was sitting in a crowded club."

"Seems to me, you've got your answer then," Banks said.

"Maybe. Maybe, not." I eyed Big Earl. "Some people might say it's awfully convenient that the victim's husband got himself such an airtight alibi, with lots of witnesses all around. Some people might say that a man with connections might have the dough and the pull to get someone else to do his wet work for him—"

"A man like my client?"

"Well, now that you mention it, yes."

Big Earl's pale face and blue eyes grew stormy. "You got a big mouth for a little woman."

"And from what I hear, you've got a small mind for a big man. But I won't hold it against you."

Big Earl's jaw tightened and his nostrils flared. "I didn't even let my Brandy talk to me like that. I sure ain't gonna let you." He took a step toward me, fists ready to strike.

Banks caught him by the elbow. "Don't," he muttered and turned to me. "Just who do you think you are?"

"I'm a reporter, like I said. And I'm just doing my job." I looked pointedly at Big Earl. "Digging beneath the surface. Bringing out the man behind the mask."

Big Earl yanked his arm free and rounded on Banks. "You better do something 'bout this woman, or I'll—"

Banks raised a calming hand. "It's okay."

"No, it ain't. It ain't nothin' near okay." Big Earl glared at me. "Brandy was my woman and I miss her. I didn't kill her. Didn't have nothing to do with it. It's that Tessie woman who took her away from me. That Tessie!"

His voice dropped low, seething with anger. "Now, I don't care nothing about her killing her man, but she–she shoulda left my Brandy alone." He clenched and unclenched his huge hands. "You gonna be seeing her again?"

"Probably."

"Tell her she better keep her ass in jail. Tell her she's safer in there than out. Cause I'll kill her if I see her. I swear I'll wring her scrawny neck."

"Thanks. That's a great quote. I'll be sure to use it for publication."

Talking about waving a red flag in front of a bull. Looking back, even I wonder what I was thinking.

Big Earl's face contorted in rage. He was about to explode.

Banks stepped in and gripped me by the elbow. "Come over here. I got words for you."

I tried to yank myself free, but he held on tight and hustled me a distance away. He loosened his grip, but he didn't let go, and leaned in close, his voice low and tense.

"Look," he said. "I get it. You don't like him—"

"Oh, I like him a lot—for this."

"You're off your rocker. The big lug didn't do it."

"Says you."

I stared at Big Earl over Banks' shoulder. Banks snapped his fingers in my face, insisting I look at him.

"He didn't do it, I tell ya. I was with him when he got the news. I ain't never seen a man cry, not like that. You can't tell 'cause you got him all riled up, but he's all broken up about it. Inside. He's a real sensitive guy."

In the background, Mr. Sensitive was pacing back and forth, pounding his gigantic fists into one another. When he caught me looking, he gave me the evil eye. I gave it right back.

"You're sweet," I told Banks, "to stand up for him. But guilty husbands have faked innocence before. They do it all the time."

"Not this guy. He didn't do it, I tell ya. For one thing, he ain't good at lying. For another, it ain't the kind of killing he'd do."

Now *that*, I admit, got my attention. Banks must've seen it in my face because he pressed on.

"Think about it," he said, "the way it was done. It's obvious. Big Earl ain't subtle—"

"There was nothing 'subtle' about it."

"Those gunshots—one to the eye, and one to the mouth—"

"How'd you know about that? The cops aren't spilling those beans."

He licked his lips uneasily. "Look, I got my sources. Anyway, I'm right, ain't I? It's not the kind a thing Big Earl would do."

"Not personally, no. But he could've paid somebody."

"Lady, lady! C'mon! I know you gotta get your story, but be fair about it."

"I'm always fair."

"Well, then listen here to what I'm telling ya: this guy, he ain't the type to kill at a distance. If he wanted that guy dead, he wouldna hired no gat. He woulda done it himself. He woulda gone over there, to that studio, and yeah, he woulda killed the guy. Sure, he woulda. But he woulda *beat* him to a pulp. And he woulda used his bare knuckles to do it."

He had a point. Mr. Sensitive over there was much more likely to pound a man into the dirt than to shoot him point-blank. His first instinct had been to use his fists when I antagonized him.

"What about Brandy?"

"Her? Sure, he woulda roughed her up a bit."

I raised an eyebrow.

"Okay," he said, "maybe more than a bit. But she woulda been alive, I tell ya. Alive! Don't you see? What he *wouldna* done—what he *wouldna* done was shoot 'em down. Not in a million years. Not *this* guy."

Him and his weasel eyes. He thought he was a smooth talker.

"So, what you're saying is this: that Big Earl is hot-headed enough to kill, just too hot-headed to have done it the way it was done."

He hesitated, as if suspecting me of trying to trick him. "Yeah," he finally said.

What a character reference! It was twisted, but maybe—I hated to admit it—just maybe that was why it rang true.

Big Earl was known for his hair-trigger temper. He was also known for using his fists to settle arguments. Sure, he had the motive to have done it, even the temperament, but would he have done it *that way*?

Another mental coin dropped.

The nude photographs implied that Andrew had died because he'd taken the wrong pictures of the wrong woman. But if they were the reason, then why were they left behind?

"So, you're gonna ease off him?"

"I'll think about it. I'll ... be fair."

"Thanks. That's all I ask."

He tipped his hat, then went back to his client to give him a reassuring pat on the shoulder.

Teddy Banks.

He was hiding something. Maybe even a couple of 'somethings.' For one thing, he knew way too much about the crime. For another, he looked plenty capable of doing such a deed himself—or of having it done. With his bloodless face and cruel lips, he was definitely the type to 'kill at a distance'—or even up close, for that matter. So, he was with Big Earl when they got the news, was he? How convenient. They could alibi each other.

Suppose Big Earl really hadn't had anything to do with the crime? Suppose it was Banks who was behind it? But why? Why would he have done such a thing? What would he have gained by it?

I couldn't see a motive behind it, not for him.

Not then.

9

September has never my favorite month. I'm owning up to that right off the bat, but I had fairly happy memories of it from when I was a kid. It was the month when the hot gritty summers ended and the cool clean weather set in. It was the start of a new school year, new books, and new adventures.

But that year, it was the start of murder, and the weather seemed to know it. Bright, crisp days leading up to the King-Sullivan killings, dark days thereafter. Everything was gray, gun-metal gray. The city was as leeched of color as a corpse, and the sky hung low, as grim as a dead man's smile.

Just go ahead and cry already, I thought, pausing to glance upward. I've never liked drizzly weather. *If you're going to rain, then rain. Do what you've got to do and get on with it.*

A single raindrop fell on the tip of my nose.

I swiped it off, climbed into my car, and pulled out into traffic. I should've been headed back up to the paper. But I had a few questions that still needed asking. That meant going back to the neighborhood where it happened.

That meant starting with Darleen's.

* * *

The Fish 'n' Fry wasn't much when it came to size or appearance, but it had good food and great prices. It had been there forever and was a favorite hang-out for the locals.

It was time for lunch. The place was busy, with Darleen hustling to serve the noonday crowd. I slid onto a stool at the counter and waited till she saw me. I didn't have to wait long. She confirmed that she'd been working the night before.

She thought she'd heard gunshots at around ten. "At the time, I thought it was a car backfiring." Other than that, she had nothing to say.

"If you come by later, though, I might have something for you."

"Like what?"

"Like Brandy's best friend, Macy Dean. She likes to stop in here before going to work. Usually drops in around six. If anybody knows anything, she does."

I thanked her, ordered coffee and a Reuben on rye, took thirty for lunch, and then headed back out into the gray.

* * *

The violence of Andrew's death had turned his place of pride into an object of morbid curiosity. The killer, whatever the motive, had stolen not only Andrew's life but his legacy.

People walking by the studio slowed down to point and stare, transfixed not by the light of the genius who had worked there, but by the darkness that had destroyed him. They stood in little clumps, whispering and shaking their heads, before moving on. They would remember Andrew not for how he'd lived and what he'd achieved but for how he had died.

That would apply to Brandy, too.

Standing on the street, thinking about Andrew, it hit me that I had forgotten about her—about Brandy, the person. I had become so focused on the murders, on unmasking her husband as a possible killer, that I had forgotten about Brandy herself. Instead of barging into J.B.'s and accusing Big Earl outright, I should've gotten him to talk about her. I'd never met her or seen her perform, and now I'd missed a golden opportunity to learn more about her, her talents, her goals, her dreams—about what we, the community, had lost in losing her.

I would begin to remedy that, when I talked to Macy Dean.

Dodging traffic, I crossed to the newsstand on the other side of the street. The dealer was a broad-shouldered, balding man in his forties, playing with a baseball. I didn't know what his full name was, but his last name was Jackson and everybody called him "Soldier." He'd had this stand for almost as long as Andrew had had his studio.

"Hi, Miss Lanie." He gave a nod toward Andrew's studio. "That sure must've been a mess in there last night. Everybody's talking about it."

"You knew him pretty well, did you?"

"Well, everybody 'round here did. Me, maybe a little more than most. We went back to the war. Fought together. Andrew," he said, "was a good man and a good friend of mine. He's the one who helped me get started in this business. If it weren't for him, I wouldn't be the businessman I am today."

"My condolences, then, on the loss of your friend."

"Thank you." He tossed the ball a little way in the air and caught it. "Heard they arrested his wife, Tessie. Pardon me for saying so, but I hope they fry her. Fry her good. Extra crispy! Shooting a good man like that, over nothing."

"So, you do think she did it?"

He paused in tossing the ball to look at me. "Course I do. She said she did, didn't she? That's what I heard."

"Do you know her, too?"

Jackson made a little grunt of pain and bent to rub his right knee.

"Arthritis?"

"Old war wound."

"Weather like this, it can't be easy."

"Nah, it ain't. But I done learned to make do."

He leaned forward across the stacks of newspapers, beckoned me to come closer and lowered his voice. "Listen, I don't want to say nothing against her. It wouldn't be right, but she shot my man down. Shot him in cold blood. So, I'm gonna say this—and I'd be willing to testify to it any damn day of the week: that is one green-eyed woman. He used to talk about her, how jealous she was. Why it was only last week he said he was wondering whether she wasn't gonna do something to him one day."

"Do something?" I dropped my voice to match his. "Like what?"

"Like *poison* him!" He gave an affirmative nod at my look of shock. "That's right. He sure did."

"He said that?"

"Close enough. Now, that's all I'm gonna say—but I think he was thinking she'd do it slow, so nobody'd notice. But she must've figured a gun was her best bet after all."

He straightened up with a self-satisfied look.

I can't say I was convinced. Not fully. And my expression must've shown it, because he shrugged and said, "You asked. I told."

"And you've told the police this?"

He nodded. "Yep."

Another nail in her coffin.

A man in a well-cut coat and business suit came up to the newsstand. Jackson greeted him with a warm smile.

"Good day, sir."

The man grabbed a copy of the *Amsterdam News,* tossed some coins Jackson's way and kept on going.

"Who the hell does he ...," Jackson muttered. His lips curled bitterly. "Some people," he said out loud, "ain't got no manners."

"I guess he was in a hurry."

"That's no excuse." Jackson stared after the stranger with narrowed eyes.

"About Andrew, did you see him yesterday?"

"'Course I did." He slowly returned his attention to me. "I saw him every day."

"About what time?"

"On and off. I saw him close up shop. Didn't notice him coming back." He bent and rubbed his knee. "I'm sorry, but I didn't see nothing worth mentioning. Not a thing."

"No strange characters lurking around the studio?"

He gave a lopsided smile. "Well, of course I did, if you put it like that. That Andrew, he had all kinds of people going in and out of there. Rich and poor. Black and white and everything in-between."

"You see Brandy's husband, Big Earl, hanging around?"

He hesitated. "No."

"You sure?"

"Yeah."

But he didn't sound sure.

I leaned in and dropped my voice. "Look, I understand. Big Earl, he can be pretty intimidating, but—"

He shook his head. "Miss Lanie, you know me. I been to hell and back. After what I went through in that war over there, don't nothing frighten me. I'm saying I ain't seen nothing 'cause I ain't seen nothing. Simple. Ain't no more to it than that."

I straightened up. "All right. But you might want to know

that my paper's putting out a reward for information leading to an arrest."

I crossed my fingers behind my back. It wasn't a lie, not quite. I hadn't spoken to Sam about a reward or anything like that, but I intended to.

He inclined his head. "How much?"

"Enough to make it worth your while."

He thought about it, then shook his head.

"Well, thank you for letting me know. But I'm not the kind of man who needs to be paid to do what's right. And Andrew ... he was special. If I knew something, then trust me, I'd be more than happy to tell you. If I do remember anything, I'll let you know."

I didn't have confidence he would. In my experience, most people who say that don't mean it. But I thanked him, gave him my card and moved on.

10

I checked the other businesses on the corner, then moved on to the street vendors, to Jimmy the 'Hot Peanuts' man and Bolo, the 'Reefer' man. I went from the numbers runner on the left to the banker on the right. They had nothing to say about the crime, but they all had something to say about Andrew, and it amounted to the same thing: that he was "one of those guys who cared."

"He had this idea about keeping track of the changes in Harlem," one said, "but he wanted to do it by focusing on regular folk."

"He said enough pictures were being taken of the prominent people," another one said. "It's the everyday people that matter. Everyday people, he said, are like the ground: strong, solid, but taken for granted. Matter-of-fact, he used to talk about how colored people, poor people, built this country, how we salted it with our sweat, fertilized it with our blood, gave our lives for it. That we a part of the bedrock of this country, and have every right to do well in it."

Apparently, Andrew had wanted to mount a show. He

even had a name for it: *A Living History: The Changing Faces of Lenox.*

"I guess that won't be happening now," said Bolo, with a sad shake of his head, a sentiment shared by everyone.

Like Darleen, they all put the shooting at ten or so. Otherwise, nobody admitted to having seen or heard a thing.

I had more than enough information for a good story, though. There was good color on Andrew that I could use to fill out his profile. But I'd have to wait till evening to learn more about Brandy.

What, I wondered, would her friend Macy Dean have to say?

* * *

I headed back to where I'd parked my car, paused on the corner to put my notepad and pencil back in my purse.

"Excuse me," a voice said.

I looked up to find a woman standing next to me. She was thin and her clothing looked worn and faded. She was probably in her thirties, but she looked fifty, aged before her time. Her face was drawn and her eyes dull with misery.

She held out a sheet of jagged-edged paper, ripped from a composition book. Instead of text, it bore a rough sketch of the head and shoulders of a young girl. She was a cute little thing. Like a doll. Could've been six or ten. From the drawing, it was hard to say.

"My baby," she said. "Her name's Cana—Cana Lee. You seen her?"

The drawing was unskilled. People who knew the child might see her in it, but a stranger probably wouldn't.

I shook my head. "I'm sorry, I—"

"You sure? Take a good look at it," she said, giving the picture a little shake under my nose.

I obliged her with another look but had to be honest. "No, I'm sorry. I just don't—"

She turned away and walked up to the next person who happened by, and got the same answer. She went from person to person, always the same question, always the same response. Most people barely glanced at the sketch. Those who did, like me, shrugged or shook their heads. Still, she kept on.

I saw her exhaustion and her worry, and it made me think of another mother, up in Hamilton Heights, who was grieving for her lost son.

For a moment, I was grateful that Hamp and I had never had a child. We'd wanted to. That's what we'd bought that big old townhouse on Strivers' Row for. But Hamp had died and now ... Well, now, I sensed that my chance had slipped by.

Sometimes, I admit it, I felt sorry for myself. But then there were other times, like this, when—thinking of Mama King, or watching that woman—I told myself I was lucky. No, I would never know the joy of loving a child, but I'd never have to live with the fear or suffer the pain of losing one, either.

You're blessed, I said. If only I felt that way.

* * *

Walking on, I focused on writing Andrew's profile in my head; I was so preoccupied with trying to get the right wording of the first paragraph, that I almost walked past an old friend.

"Hey, beautiful!"

I turned to see the grizzled old face of a shoeshine man. "Roy!" I smiled. "How you doing?"

His face split into a wide grin. "I'm fine and you? I ain't seen you in a while. Ain't that something with this King business?"

"Did you know him?"

"Knew him? Why I was talking to him just yesterday. It

was just about 'round about this time. He was all excited. Said he was gonna have a big meeting last night."

At first, I assumed Roy meant Brandy, but then something dawned on me. Would Andrew have referred to his appointment with her as a 'big meeting?' Would he have even mentioned the appointment to someone else? That would've been untoward. It could've cost him future business.

Having seen those pictures of Brandy, I now wondered whether Andrew hadn't taken similar pictures of others, at their request. It could've been a lucrative sideline, a select addition to his more traditional services. If so, he could've only succeeded if he'd been discreet, if his clients had trusted him.

Had he taken other pictures, of someone who had regretted the decision to have the images made, someone who feared he wouldn't stay silent and had moved to silence him? Had Andrew given this person a good reason to fear him? Had he himself tried to blackmail someone?

It was an ugly thought. I didn't want to entertain it, but once it presented itself, it was persistent. It wouldn't go away. I had to look it in the face and—

"A meeting?" I asked, drawing closer. "Did he say with whom?"

"Well, you know he had this hope of putting on a show, right?"

I blinked. My mind had gotten so wrapped up with thoughts of blackmail that I was surprised at this reference to the show.

"Yes," I said, "go on."

"So, Andrew, he wanted to put his pictures up where everybody could see 'em. He must've got a bead on one of them white folk who pay for that kind of thing. Said he'd met somebody who was gonna hook him up and they was all gonna meet that night."

Now fully focused on what Roy was saying, I leaned in. "He mention a name?"

"Just said he was gonna meet this white guy."

Was this a possible witness? Or maybe the killer himself? "Did you tell the police any of this?"

"Nope. They ain't asked."

I thanked him and headed back to my car. Along the way, I stopped off at a drug store to pick up a small bar of perfumed soap, a toothbrush and toothpaste, and a clean handkerchief. The store was kind enough to wrap them in some pretty paper and fold it so it would stay closed.

In the back of my mind, I was turning over Roy's information. It was good info and I was glad he'd told me. The question was how to use it?

How to find this phantom backer, who no one else had mentioned and for whom I had no name?

11

Nella Harding was a white socialite, music columnist and photography enthusiast. An avid party-goer, she had a range of contacts in New York's arts and entertainment world who kept her abreast of the doings uptown in Harlem as well as downtown in Greenwich Village.

If anyone could find that backer, she could.

Once back at my desk in the newsroom, I had the exchange put in a call.

She had heard of the double murders, of course, and the arrest of Andrew's wife. She had, "met Andrew several times, at parties," she said.

"Tessie's not much to look at, but that man—oh, that man was gorgeous, darling. I would've done him in a minute, given half the chance. Just between us, I actually tried. But he was all about his Tessie. He thought the world of her. To think she would gun him down like that."

I could just about feel her shaking her head.

"And then, there's Brandy," she went on. "I loved her. Those incredible long legs! What a dancer! She could sing, too. I think she was well on her way to becoming a headliner. I so enjoyed seeing her perform." A sigh. "I don't know what she saw in that big lug of hers—another case of Beauty and the Beast, I guess."

Another deep sigh. "I was really heartbroken to hear of it. All of it. Brandy and Andrew and Tessie. What a waste of life, of talent and potential!"

She paused. "But you don't really think Tessie did it, do you? I mean, that's why you're calling, isn't it?"

I smiled into the phone. "You know me too well."

* * *

Right after getting off the phone, I got a note that Tessie had tried to reach me. There was no explanation of why. Being a worrywart, I immediately feared the worst, that she'd found a way to do something to herself.

I had the exchange call the jailhouse, but to my utter frustration, no one answered. I threw on my coat, grabbed my purse and headed back downtown.

The courthouse jailer looked surprised to see me.

"No, nothing's happened to her," he said when I asked him whether she was all right. "Well, I wouldn't say she's exactly doing fine," he added. "She's been crying a lot, and refusing her meals and water. If she don't start cooperating, we're going to have to force-feed her."

"You wouldn't."

"Oh, yes, ma'am. We would."

"Take me down to see her."

Tessie looked paler and even thinner than before. Her face was swollen; her eyes were lackluster and rimmed with dark circles. She looked surprised and overjoyed to see me —*to see anyone*, I thought, *who didn't assume she was guilty.*

"Oh, I didn't mean for you to come all the way down here," she said. "Not twice in one day."

"I got your message and I was worried."

The jailer let me into the cell. As before, Tessie and I sat on the edge of her bunk bed.

"You've got to take better care of yourself," I told her. "Here, I brought you a little care package." It was just the items I'd picked up after talking to Roy.

She smiled gratefully, then covered her eyes, bent her head, and repressed a sob. I wrapped my arms around her and gave her a hug. I wished I could tell her it was going to be all right, but I couldn't. She used the handkerchief to dry her face and found her voice.

"Mama King," she sniffed. "That's why I called. I just wanted to know. How is she? You did go to see her, right?"

"She's ... Let's just say, she's as well as can be expected."

Tessie sighed. "She doesn't deserve this. Maybe, it would be better if I just let go. If I ..."

"Let go? What do you mean by that?"

Her eyes filled with tears, and her voice grew thick.

"Not fight, anymore. Just let them take me, do with me what they mean to. Cause you and I both know, they're never going to let me out of here. The trial ... it'll just make everything worse for her. If I say I did it, then it'll be over. Mama King could bury her son, forget about me, and move on."

"Do you really think she wants you to do that?"

Tessie swallowed, shrugged. "No. I don't know. I guess not. It's just that ..." She gazed out past the bars. "I loved him, you know? I really, really loved him, with all my heart and soul. I was always so scared of losing him. And now I have."

"Yes, and that's a mighty deep hurt, but you haven't lost everything. You're young and you could—"

"Find love again?" She gave a rueful little laugh. "We both know that's not going to happen. I'm well aware that I'm not the prettiest apple on the tree. Everybody used to point that out to me. But not Andrew. He was always telling me how beautiful I was. 'You such a liar,' I used to say. But the fact was, I really think he meant it. He saw me with different eyes. He liked me. He actually liked me."

She shook her head as if she still couldn't understand it. "Most people don't. I know that. They say I'm arrogant and cold, and I guess I can be that way. But with Andrew, it was different. *I* was different. Nicer. I—"

She caught herself, closed her eyes, was still for a moment, and then opened them again. "I'm sorry. I know you didn't come here to hear me rattle on like this."

"Actually..."

Sam had suggested doing a piece that would balance out the editorial. *"Talk to her, Lanie. Draw her out. Let's paint a picture of a human being, someone our readers can relate to."*

"Tessie, I would like to share your story, the story of you and Andrew."

"Of me and ...?"

"Of how you met and fell in love, of what your marriage meant to you."

She drew back. "No, no I can't do that. I won't. My story with Andrew—it's the last thing I have of him, of what was ours. And the idea of letting you use it—to sell papers, to—"

"To save your life. That's what this is all about. Saving your life. Nothing more—and certainly nothing less."

She held my gaze, her forehead puckered in doubt and worry.

"Tessie, don't you think it's time your story was told in your words, from your point of view? Up till now, all anybody's heard is innuendo and gossip."

"But—"

"You do realize, don't you, that there's a mob out there, ready to crucify you? And I'm not talking about a white one, but a colored one. I'm talking about *us*, our own people. The folks are *angry*. Andrew was a shining light of hope to so many of them, and now they think you took him away. They *blame* you. If there was ever a time to lift that veil, to share your life, this is it. Think about it. Please."

She worried her lower lips. She shook her head. "I'm sorry. I can't."

"Not even if it means saving your own life?"

"Not even. It's something ... special. The only thing I got special left. It was his gift to me and I won't ..."

"You're thinking you don't want to cheapen it by ..."

"Yes."

I took a moment, trying to figure out how to reach her, to get through.

"Don't you think it's possible to tell your story in a way that honors it, honors Andrew?"

She got up and paced the floor, twisting and rubbing her hands together. Finally, she came to a stop and studied me, her dark eyes questioning.

"I want to trust you, but ... Tell me, do you believe in me, believe I'm innocent?"

"I was wondering when you'd ask me that."

"And what's your answer?"

"That I don't know. I am not sure. I do know that Mama King deserves better than to have her son gunned down and see the wrong person sent to jail. She deserves justice. And she loves you. She asked me to do what I could to make sure you have a fair trial. I said I would. And I'm going to."

She pressed her eyes closed. Heavy tears rolled down her thin cheeks and she didn't bother to wipe them away.

I softened my voice. "Tessie, I understand that you don't know who to trust, and I respect that. All I can say is, whatever you decide, don't give up hope. It's just too early for that."

She licked her lips. "OK. What do you want to know?"

"Come. Sit down and talk to me. Tell me how you and Andrew got together."

She swallowed and eased down on the bed next to me.

"Try to remember back, beyond these four walls," I said gently. "Go back to the good times."

She smiled at that and inclined her head, reflecting.

The lights in the cell flickered and dimmed, creating shadows that made the walls close in. I could understand why Tessie would begin to feel despair, locked up in a municipal dungeon, unable to grieve the loss of the man she loved.

And there's no doubt that she did indeed love him. The problem was that love is no proof of innocence. Killers so often love the ones they kill and kill the ones they love. But somehow, I still felt that her love story would humanize her. It would simply be a matter of striking the right balance in telling it.

"We met at a bus stop. It was November, a really gloomy day—sort of like yesterday, actually—and it began raining. He had an umbrella and I didn't, so he invited me to stand with him under his. Of course, I said, 'No, no way,' but he kept at it. Pretty soon, he had me laughing and ... well, it went on from there."

The courtship that followed was bittersweet.

"I tried every which way to dissuade him. I never intended to get married. All I ever wanted to do was write. That's all I've ever dreamed of, is to be an author, and I didn't need no man at home expecting me to wait on him hand and foot—or to break me with heartache."

She paused at that. Was she thinking of how heartache had found her despite all her attempts to avoid it?

"But when I met Andrew," she went on, "something changed. It was as if something woke up inside me. I saw that, yes, I wanted to write, but I wanted to be a wife and mother, too—a wife to this man, the mother of his children.

"Then came the day when Andrew said he wanted me to meet his mother. I knew it was getting serious, that if I was going to bail out, I had to do it right then and there. 'Cause he was a good man. I could see that. And he didn't need to be strung along. I thought about it long and hard and I decided I wouldn't go with him, that it was time to end it, that in fact, all those things I now thought I wanted was just me being mixed up by love. It was exactly the kind of 'distraction' I'd known all along would be dangerous. And here I was, about to fall into the trap Mama had warned me against."

"Your *mother?*"

"Oh, yeah. She was as frustrated as they come. Wanted to be a biologist—"

"Really?"

"Hm-hmm. She was smart and she just loved science. But then my daddy came along and he told her that she'd never make it. That the world wasn't ready for a colored woman scientist. I'm not sure she ever believed him, but she let him persuade her to marry him. Not soon after she had me, he died."

Tessie's voice was calm, but heavy with memories. "Mama gave up on her dreams, but she never forgot about them. And she traced the turning point in her life to her meeting my father."

Tessie's gave another bitter slight half-smile. "My mother wasn't happy being a mother. She tried her best, but it just wasn't in her."

She appeared to be lost in thought for a moment, then roused herself and smiled gamely. "I just knew I wasn't going to be like her. My situation was going to be different. And I guess it is. It actually turned out to be worse. Not only is my husband dead, but I'm accused of having killed him." She gave a snort and a chuckle, covering her mouth and shaking her head. "It would all be so damned funny if it weren't so …" She sniffed. "I'm sorry."

"No, it's OK."

She nodded, biting down on her lower lip.

"So, what happened," I asked. "Obviously, you agreed to meet his mother."

"Yes … Obviously, I did. I just couldn't say, 'No,' to that man. I never could. But I warned him. She wasn't going to like me. I just knew it. They never do, right? And in my case, I wasn't pretty and my cooking wasn't worth a da—well, let's just say it wasn't there. I wasn't interested in cooking or cleaning or in mending her boy's shirts. I didn't see myself doing any of the million and one things women are supposed to *want* to do. That was not me.

"But that was her. From what Andrew told me, that was clearly her. And sure enough, I recognized her type the moment I met her. Neat as pin; everything in its place, dinner on the table every day, same time, warm and delicious, the table perfectly laid out. Not like me at all."

I had to smile to myself. I knew what Tessie was saying. I would've had the same fear meeting my husband's mother if it hadn't been for the fact that he and I had grown up knowing each other, with my father working in his family's household. Even so, when the time came for us to announce our engagement, I'd been afraid that his family would oppose it. After all, his people were well-heeled and mine were not. We came from different sides of the tracks. But they had taken it well, and from what I could see in Tessie's case, the meeting had gone well, too.

"I used to say to him, 'With a mama like that, why would you want a woman like me?' And he'd laugh and say, 'That's exactly why I want you—well, one reason, anyway. And then he'd hug me and make me feel loved." She paused.

"I loved him. I would've died for him. Easy. The fact that he's gone—and the way he was taken—sometimes the pain is so sharp I can't breathe. How could anyone think I'd do that to him? He was the answer to dreams I didn't even know I had."

She smiled with forced confidence. "And that's what I'm going to tell the court. When my trial comes, I'll explain how much I loved him and how I never could've done anything to harm him. And they'll understand. Don't you think they'll understand?"

"Yes, of course, they will."

I had thought myself so smart, so clever, in seizing upon her love story with Andrew. I hadn't thought it through. Now, as I listened to her, it occurred to me that, too often, declarations of love have led not to an acquittal but a conviction.

It had become clear that her love for Andrew could be used against her. A prosecutor could say that her devotion wasn't just passionate but desperate. He would point to it as a motive for murder, especially since jealousy had come into play. How many people have killed the man or woman they loved? Too many. That's all the prosecutor would have to say. If I wrote about their love story, would I be supporting the prosecution—or would I be helping ensure that she got a fair trial, that her words and thoughts, her intentions and feelings, weren't twisted to satisfy the public's thirst for revenge and a prosecutor's ambitions for a quick win?

"So, tell me about you and Mama King. What happened when you finally met her?"

"It was just as you'd expect. We were polite and cautious. I don't think she approved of me, but odd as it sounds, I don't think she disapproved, either. She gave herself time, time to get to know me, time for me to get to know her. She talked to me and she listened when I talked to her. And she surprised me. She read my books. She gave me good advice—"

"About writing?"

"About life. And about Andrew. It hit me one day that she really wanted it to work out between us. Then came the day when she told me she would've never foreseen Andrew bringing home someone like me. But, now that she'd gotten to know me, she was glad he had."

"'Someone like you?' What did that mean?"

She frowned. "Funny. I never asked her. I guess I just assumed she meant a plain Jane like me, and someone so different from her."

I thought about it. "OK. Go on."

"There's really not much more to say. I've come to love her. She's been more than fair to me. I know that whatever kindness she's shown toward me was maybe for the sake of her son, but I–I love her. In some ways, she's been the mother I never had. I never would've hurt her by taking her son away. And I would do anything now to ease her pain." Her expression grew resolved. "Anything."

"No, Tessie, no. Your confessing to something you didn't do wouldn't help her. It wouldn't help anybody—but the killer. It would just make sure that he goes free. Do you want that?"

She pressed her lips tight and shook her head, no, but I wasn't so sure I'd convinced her.

It was only after leaving Tessie that I remembered what I'd forgotten to ask her.

12

I t was supper time, by then. Time to go back over to the Fish 'n' Fry and see a dancer named Macy Dean.

When I got there, Darleen pointed out a thin slip of a girl sitting in the back at a corner table.

"She won't talk to you out in the open. You can meet in the kitchen."

Over the next hour or so, I didn't eat, but I did have a good listen, 'cause Macy Dean sure had a tale to tell.

She confirmed that Brandy had gone to Andrew to have the pictures done for Big Earl, and absolutely denied the existence of any romance between Brandy and Andrew.

"Believe it or not, she only had eyes for that big lug." Did Big Earl know about the pictures?

Macy wasn't sure. They were for his birthday. Brandy meant to surprise him.

So, if Big Earl found out about the visits to Andrew's studio before he was meant to, he might've misinterpreted them?

"Well, he did find out."

"Come again?"

The night before, when Big Earl stopped by Small's, he saw that Brandy wasn't there.

"I told him she'd mentioned having to stop by Andrew's."

"Did he threaten you?"

"He didn't have to. Everybody's scared of him–him and that crooked manager of his. There's no way I was gonna cross them for her."

She hugged herself and gave a little shiver. Briefly, I wondered what had motivated her to talk to me if she was so afraid of crossing Big Earl and Banks. I asked her.

She shrugged. "Guilt, I guess," she said after a moment. "If I hadn't told him where to find her, then …"

I nodded—I could understand her feeling that way—and moved on. "What's the feeling at the Cotton Club?"

"We pretty broken up about it. Brandy had a good heart. When she first joined us, you know most of us didn't trust her. I mean, we're all kind of cute, but Brandy was … amazing. One bat of her lashes, one glance from her hazel eyes, and the men would come a'running. So, we all thought what people think when they see a woman with looks like that, that she's after everybody's man. But Brandy wasn't like that. For one thing, she was a church girl. She was in church every Sunday and read her Bible before going to work every night. I ain't lying. She coulda had just about any man she wanted. But all she wanted was Big Earl." Macy shook her head. "We couldn't none of see why. At first, we thought it was maybe the money he was earning. But then …"

She shrugged.

"Then what?" I asked.

She eyed me, as if considering something, then leaned in and whispered "You a reporter, right?"

"Yes."

"Well, if I tell you something, then can you keep it a secret? Or do you got to write everything you hear?"

"No, I can choose. We can, as we say, talk off the record."

"And that means you won't say nothing 'bout what I say?"

"I means that I will use your information, but I'll never say who gave it to me."

"Never?"

"Never."

She mulled that over. "Look, I'm not *asking* for money, you understand, but …"

"How much?"

She gave an exaggerated shrug. "I don't know. Maybe a *grand*?"

"For that sister, you'd have to deliver the killers hogtied in a barrel. How about a C-note?"

She pursed her lips and looked downright unhappy, but we both knew it was a good amount of change.

"When?" she said finally.

"Right now." I had anticipated this and pulled two fifties from my wallet. I handed her the first one. "Now, spill."

She made those berries disappear faster than I could blink.

"Big Earl's stash had dried up. He wasn't getting the big purses no more. Brandy told me he was under pressure to throw his next fight."

"You haven't told me anything I couldn't guess."

"Well, I bet you didn't guess that she's the one done talked him out of taking a dive the last time and that she was trying to talk him out of it again."

She paused to see if this was news to me. It was, but I kept my poker face on. I could see where she was going and it was making my stomach tight.

"I told her it was dangerous. She said she knew, and that Teddy Banks had been breathing down her neck. Said he told her that if she didn't shut up, she'd get 'em all iced. That last fight, the one that Big Earl *didn't* throw? That was in the ring with Madden's man, one of his fighters."

"So, Big Earl had agreed to lose and—"

"Yeah, he won instead. I told Brandy it was amazing she was still living. I mean, you know who Madden is, don't you? You don't cross him. You do and you end up dead-like Battling Siki. You remember him, don't you?"

Who could forget?

It had been two years since the Senegalese boxer was found murdered. Two years and the killer was still free. Siki was slain during the early hours of a December morning, ambushed on a filthy street in Hell's Kitchen.

The U.S. papers were quick to blame him, practically said he had it coming. After all, he was known for drinking and brawling, wasn't he? No doubt, he'd picked a fight with the wrong person. Never mind that no one had seen him involved in any brawls or arguments that night. That didn't matter. It was Siki's own fault he ended up face down in the gutter, shot in the back.

The European papers took a different view, one that was probably closer to the truth: that there was a fix, and that Siki hadn't gone along with it, or had done a double-cross. And someone somewhere had settled the score, the "someone" being Madden.

"Big Earl's got another fight coming up," Macy said. "This one's supposed to be for big money. Brandy said he told her that if he did this next one, he'd never have to throw another fight. That there'd be enough to go around, enough to keep the mob happy and let him retire. But Brandy wasn't having it. She wanted him out. Pronto. Like yesterday."

She lit herself a cigarette.

"You ask how it is over at the Club? It's bad. How do you think we feel when we know we got a killer for a boss?"

"But do you think he had a hand in this one?"

"*Think?* We don't just think. We pretty damn sure. Andrew's wife? She didn't have nothing to do with it. It was Madden—him or Big Frenchy or one of his other men. It really don't matter. You just need to know that they stepped in. They stepped in and took care of business."

13

I helped Sam carry out the plates to my dining room table. I was not the one who had done the cooking that night. Sam enjoyed preparing meals and he loved my kitchen. That night, he'd prepared a meal of baked macaroni, green salad, and sweet potato pie. I was supplying the wine.

I hadn't said anything about my talk with Macy Dean during the meal preparation because I wanted Sam's full attention. But after we sat down, and said grace, I began.

He listened intently, as he always did, only interrupting once or twice to clarify something. After I was done, he was pensive.

"For a while there, there was a lot of talk going around that Big Earl was throwing fights. There was that fight—about three months ago—all of us, we were pretty sure we knew what would happen: Big Earl would dance a little, throw a few soft jabs to put on a good show, maybe even land a punch or two, but nothing hard, mind you. Nothing real. And then he'd take a fall in the fourth—cause he's done it before. And, at first, it really did look like he was keeping his head down, doing nothing. But then, all of a sudden, he came out, charging like a bull. It was the Big Earl we knew. He was back, just like that. And let me tell you, it was like night and day."

"So, you agree. You think Banks arranged for Big Earl to take a fall—"

"I think Big Earl entered that ring, intending to take a dive, but something stopped him. He couldn't go through with it. To tell you the truth, a lot of us were waiting to see, expecting to see—some kind of after-the-show fireworks, if you get my meaning. Cause you don't agree to take a fall—*if* that's what it was—and get to just walk away from it."

"But you're saying nothing happened?"

"Nothing…till maybe last night."

From the very beginning, we had all assumed that the killing had been motivated by jealousy. I realized now that as much as I had resisted the idea of Tessie's guilt, I had gone along with the theory that the rage of a cheated spouse had been the driving force behind the murders. Hence, my interest in Big Earl.

But if that wasn't the motive …

I thought of Andrew. *Were you really simply in the wrong place at the wrong time?*

The irony of it. It was *his* studio, *his* place of business where they'd died. You'd think that if anyone would've been in the wrong place at the wrong time, it would've been Brandy.

Sam continued. "Big Earl wouldn't have been the only fighter to meet a suspicious end. Within the last two years, Harry Grew, Tiger Flowers and Pancho Villa, all died of an overdose of ether while undergoing surgery. Of course," he shrugged, "since it occurred in a hospital setting, with a doctor right there, nobody took a closer look, and everybody knows that accidents can happen. However...." he raised an eyebrow.

"There's no such thing as coincidence. Three world boxing champions—"

"Two of whom we know had gotten caught up in fixing fights—"

"All dying the same way within two years of each other?" He tucked into the macaroni. "Then there was Flower's manager, Walk Miller."

"Something happened to him, too?"

"Miller was unhappy with the circumstances surrounding Flowers' death. Word is Miller was threatening to talk, to lay it out there, about the fights and the fixes. Next thing you know, he's dead, too. Beaten and shot."

"Unsolved?"

"Unsolved. So, yeah, there's reason to wonder whether Madden is involved in this mess." He was silent for several seconds. "I was just thinking of that last fight."

"Macy said he was supposed to have thrown it."

"It was the fight with Jimmy "Bad Boy" Francis. That was only three days ago—"

"Right before the killings."

"Francis is one of Madden's boys. He's green, but he's got potential and the clubs down on Broadway have been promoting him like crazy. That bout should've lasted a good long time, enough for Francis to show that he has the goods. But Big Earl played with him, then knocked him out for the count. He stood over him, and pumped his fists in the air."

"That probably pleased the crowds—"

"Oh, they roared. But the promoters were less than happy."

"And Madden must've been fit to be tied."

"Could be it. That Big Earl crossed the line," Sam said. "You planning on sharing any of this with Blackie?"

"I'm not sure."

"Because you don't think he'll listen?"

"I have my doubts, yes."

"Try it, anyway. We need to get his reaction on the record." He paused. "And then the cops can never accuse us of playing unfair."

14

The killer had 'made her eat the gun.' Isn't that what Winslow, the medical examiner, said?

The image of Brandy's damaged but still sweet face rose before my eyes.

You were the true target, weren't you?

And now I knew why.

If the mob had killed Brandy and Andrew, it would explain the placement of the gunshots. They were mob signatures.

I had started out thinking that Andrew was the target, that Brandy had either been secondary or simply in the wrong place at the wrong time. Now, it appeared that it was the other way around.

Macy Dean's information kept me up all night. It gave me my first real hope of proving to Blackie that he should look elsewhere for the killer. Maybe, just maybe, this info might even get Tessie freed.

Early the next morning, as soon as I got to the newsroom, I put in a call to Blackie. "Listen, I—"

"I'm kind of glad you called," he said. "I was going to call you. I thought you should know." He paused. "Tessie's confessed."

"She *what?!*"

"She's admitted to everything."

I gripped my desk and sank down in my chair. "But why? Why would she *do* that?"

But even as I asked, I recalled her words. *"I would do anything now to ease her pain,"* she'd said. *"Anything."*

My thoughts flew to that little old lady in Harlem Heights, who was waiting for me to bring her good news. What would I tell her? What could I say?

"Look, Lanie, I know you feel bad about this, and I don't want to rub your nose in it. But she's guilty and she knows we've got the goods on her."

My thoughts snapped back to the moment. *"What* goods?"

There was a tense silence.

"Oh, no," I breathed. "You didn't. Tell me you didn't tell her you found her fingerprints on the gun."

He didn't answer. He didn't have to.

"And did you?" I asked. "Find them?"

He cleared his throat. "The prints, they, uh ... they were smudged."

"So, the results weren't definite—"

"Lanie, she did it to herself."

"Because you lied to her."

"I did what I had to do."

His tone dared me to argue. I wasn't about to. It would've been a waste of my time.

"There's always been one thing I admired and respected about you, John Blackie, and that was your honesty. That even when dealing with suspects, you could be trusted to play it straight."

"You were naive," he said wearily. "You always have been."

"What does that mean?"

"It means that you've seen enough, been around long enough, to know better."

That stung.

"That was a low blow, but you know what? I agree. I should've known better. What was I thinking, trusting a cop? Cause you're all the same, right? Even you. Well, thank you for setting me straight. This is one lesson I will never forget."

"Oh, Lanie. C'mon. You know, I—" Conversation over. I put down the receiver.

Fuming, I realized I hadn't told him what Macy Dean had said. I picked up the handset to have the operator call him back, then lowered it again.

What good would it do? His mind was made up.

And now, so was mine.

* * *

"Oh, my God!" Tessie cried. Her hand flew to cover her mouth. Her wide eyes searched mine.

"But that detective, he told me ... he said—"

"He lied."

"Oh, my God," she repeated in a whisper. "But yes, I see," she nodded to herself. "I see what they did. They'd been leaving me alone. But then—it was right after you left here—they came in and—"

She rubbed her forehead. "They got me in that room and they kept at me. They kept saying they'd found my fingerprints on that gun, kept telling me I should just give in and say it was mine, or Andrew's. That it would save Mama King the shame of a trial. I didn't want to. I tried not to. But after a while, I got tired. Oh, you just can't imagine! I got so tired. I would've said anything to get them to stop, to let me be. So, I did it. I said it was Andrew's gun."

And from there it was a short hop to 'admitting' that she had used said gun on Andrew and Brandy.

"The gun ... *is* it his?"

"I don't know. I don't know guns. Can't tell one from another. They said it was a gun from the war. Andrew had a gun, but he said he got it from his daddy. He tried to show it to me, but I wouldn't look at it, much less touch it. I never wanted anything to do with guns. Still don't."

I know I should've felt sympathy for her. But I was too angry. For some reason, I felt as though I was the one who'd been tricked and betrayed and stabbed in the back. Wrong of me, I know. But there it was.

"Tessie, I have to know: What were you asking forgiveness for?"

Shame filled her eyes.

"I know about the argument," I said. "Mama King told me."

She was quiet for a while. Then she said, "Yes, I thought she would."

She averted her eyes and pressed her lips together. "I made a mistake. I should've had faith in him. After he left, I thought about what he said and I—I got worried. Maybe, he'd leave me. I waited a while, hoping he'd cool down. Then I called the studio. And he was there. It was around eight, maybe a quarter past. He wasn't angry anymore, but he was still hurting. He said he didn't have time to talk."

"Was someone else there?"

"I don't know. He didn't say. But I guess ... well, I guess *she* was, that dancer, that Brandy Sullivan."

Tessie said she'd laid down. When she woke up, it was after nine o'clock, "maybe half past, and Andrew still wasn't home." She called the studio, but got no answer, so she went looking for him. She stopped by a couple of the speakeasies that dotted the way to his studio, but no one had seen him.

Then she went to the studio.

"I don't remember calling the police. I barely remember them coming."

"You didn't call them. Somebody else did."

She regarded me blankly. "Somebody else?"

"Yes. It was a man. He didn't give his name."

"Oh." She thought about it, puzzled, then asked. "But how did he know? That something had happened, I mean?"

"Police said he heard you crying."

She almost smiled at that. "You mean somebody, 'specially in *that* neighborhood, called the police 'cause they heard a woman crying?"

She was right. It *was* absurd when put in that light.

I thought about it. "Well, maybe he came in and checked on you and—"

"No," she said. "I'd remember that."

She'd just said she didn't even remember the police coming in.

"If you didn't kill him, then what were you asking forgiveness for?"

She took a deep breath. "For not having had faith in him. For causing him to be there. I thought he'd run out to get away from me. Then, when I found him with Brandy, I thought he'd gone to meet her. Either way, it's my fault. If I'd given him what he needed, he would've been home, with me. Not dead on the floor. Killed by her crazy husband."

"Well, you can stop thinking that," I said. "You had nothing to do with him being there. He had an appointment with her. To give her those pictures, pictures she'd asked him to take as a gift for her husband."

Her face showed surprise—and relief. "Are you sure?"

"Very sure. They weren't having an affair, and Andrew would've been there even if you hadn't had that fight."

The guard came up. "Visiting time's over."

I said my goodbyes and promised to come back to see her, then stepped outside her cell.

Tessie gripped the bars and pressed her face against them.

"Miss Lanie, could you please go see that judge, talk to him, get him to let me out of here, just for a morning? I need to go to Andrew's funeral. To say good-bye to him, right and proper. Would you ask him for me?"

"I don't know, Tessie. I—"

"Please?"

I wanted to help her. God knows I did. But I didn't think my intervening with the judge would make things better. It might even make them worse.

"You need a lawyer," I said. "Someone to fight for you with all he's got."

"No." She shook her head. "I don't know any, and even if I did, I don't think any of them would want to defend me. Won't nobody stand up for me—nobody with any integrity that is—not with what I'm accused of having done."

I almost smiled at that. She didn't know lawyers.

15

B efore leaving the courthouse, I ducked into a phone booth to call Blackie.

"It's me," I said. "I'd like one of your photographs."

"Of what?"

"The gun.'"

"Normally, we don't give those out."

"Well, normally," I said thoughtfully, "I don't write stories about how cops work cases. But you know what? I guess I could make an exception with this one, write about how a certain detective broke *this* particular case."

Anyone else would've taken that statement as a compliment. Blackie knew better.

"You wouldn't write about what I told Tessie?"

"You mean about how you lied to her?"

"It's a method, tried and true. And you're not to write about it."

"Why not?"

"Because it's investigative method. Furthermore, everybody knows ..."

His voice trailed away as he realized what he was about to say.

"Everybody knows what, detective? That the police lie?"

I waited. We both knew that the police were already under close scrutiny for the beating death of a young colored man in Blackie's station. The papers were full of it. The community was sick of it. Something like this, even when it involved a figure as ill-perceived as Tessie, would not go down well.

"When do you need it?" he asked.

"Fifteen minutes."

* * *

I motored up East 125th Street, then headed west across town, and turned right on Sixth Avenue. I might not have noticed the car if I hadn't had to stop for the light on the south side of West 127th. That left me with a clear view of the entrance to J.B.'s Gym.

It was a black Buick, parked right out in front, just as big and bold as you please. Or maybe it wasn't a Buick. Hamp used to tease me about how much I didn't know about cars. I told him I knew all I needed to know. And right then, sitting across from J.B.'s, I didn't need to know the model or the maker to know that this was a rich man's car. And not just any rich man. Maybe it was the curtained windows. Maybe, it was the gun embrasures. But something about that baby said "bullet-proofed."

Everything about it said 'mobster.'

Sure enough, a couple of machine-gun-toting thugs emerged from J.B.'s. Seconds later, Owney Madden came strolling out. He was tossing a dime, as cool as a cucumber. He was a tight-lipped, hawk-nosed character, known for his gentle smile and cunning cruelty. His number two man, George "Big Frenchy" DeMange, rolled out behind him. Big

Frenchy was heavyset and pugnacious-looking, with beetle brows, a bulbous nose and thin lips.

Big Frenchy cast a quick glance around, just to check out his surroundings. He slid down into the back passenger seat, joining Madden. There was a flash of pale skin as Madden drew back the curtain, peeped out, then let it drop as the car pulled away.

Someone honked behind me, startling me. I glanced up, saw that the light had changed and started forward again.

Owney Madden. Big Frenchy. What business had they been taking care of inside that gym?

It could've been something as innocent as Madden conveying his condolences for Big Earl's loss. Then again, it could've been about something as dirty as putting in for the big fix.

Or it could've been about both.

Either way, it provided food for thought.

16

B lackie was out on another case when I got to the station, but he had left the photo in an envelope with Wilkins at the front desk.

I picked it up and headed over to Mama King's. A young woman in her twenties answered the doorbell. Her name was Gladys Little. She was one of the neighbors I'd talked to earlier. Her eyes widened at the sight of me and she gave me a warm smile.

"Miss Price! Why, it's so nice to see you again." She welcomed me in. "Me and some of the others, we been taking turns stopping by to see her, coordinating with Mrs. Dill." Some of the joy left her voice. "I'm so glad to see you. Your coming the last time meant a lot to her."

She led me into the living room where Mama King sat in a small armchair, reading her bible.

"Mama King," Gladys said, as she sailed into the room. "Look who I have here."

Mama King's face brightened and she started to rise.

"No, please, don't bother," I said. Gladys asked me if I

wanted anything to drink, some water or tea. I thanked her, but said no.

"OK," she said, "then I'll leave you two alone."

"Oh, please don't go on account of me."

She lowered her voice. "I was 'bout to leave, anyway. Mama King don't like having people flitting round her all the time. It's a bit much for her and she needs her privacy. So, we come in, stay a little, do a little, then let her be."

She smiled reassuringly. "Don't worry. We going to take good care of her."

She gave me a pat on the wrist, then turned back to Andrew's mother. "Mama King, if you need anything, you let me know, y'hear? Suzy Atwater'll be over in 'bout an hour, all right?"

"It's all very kind," Mama King said, "but it's not necessary—"

"Of course, it is!"

Gladys gave the old woman a hug, then hurried out, sending me a brief smile on her way out the door.

Mama King gestured for me to take a seat. She had a little tremor in her right hand that I hadn't noticed before.

"So," she said, conspiratorially, "have you got something for me? Some news? Some truth?"

"Well, I do have some news, but ... first I'd like you to answer one question for me."

"All right," she frowned.

"Did Andrew ever talk to you about having found a backer, some white fellow who was going to put up the cash for an exhibit?"

Her frown deepened. She thought about it, then slowly shook her head. "No, he never said a thing. Why? Is it important?"

"It could be."

I felt my own eyebrows draw together in a worried knot and rubbed my forehead to ease the winkles away.

"You said you have news," she said.

"Yes. You may hear it on the radio soon." I paused. "Tessie's confessed."

She stiffened. "She-she *what?!*"

I explained what happened.

"Lord, lord, lord," she shook her head. "You saying she did that to protect me? How could she think that—? What can we do? What can *I* do?"

"Actually, I do have something ... quite difficult to ask of you."

"Will it help with finding out who hurt my son, and that girl?"

"Yes, ma'am. I think so."

"All right, then."

I took out the police photo.

"What is that?" She leaned forward to get a look.

"I'm sorry," I said, and placed the picture of the gun before her.

She drew back, and her hand went to cover her heart. "Is that ... is that what I think it is?"

Her lips parted in horror. Tears entered her eyes. She squeezed them shut and pressed her lips together. Her pain was evident, but so was her resolve. After several seconds, she composed herself, reached out and took up the picture with trembling hands.

"So, this is the gun, the one that ..."

"They believe so, yes."

She studied it for several long seconds, then put it down and looked up at me.

"And what do you want to know from me?"

"This is the gun the police got Tessie to say was Andrew's."

"No," she shook her head. "That is most definitely not Andrew's gun."

I felt my heart lift a little, felt a little tug of hope. "How can you be so sure?"

"Because Andrew's gun was bigger and it had a different handle, a wooden handle. His father gave it to him."

"You're sure?"

"Oh, yes," she nodded.

"Then where is Andrew's gun?"

Was it in the studio, I wondered, *waiting to be found?*

She thought about it for a minute, then got up and went out. She returned several minutes later holding an old leather bound box. She set it on the table, then stood back, and nodded toward it, gesturing for me to open it.

Inside was a gun, all right. I didn't know much about weaponry, either, but I could clearly recognize the basket-pattern wood grip. I didn't touch the gun, just looked it over, then closed the case.

I wished I could say I felt better. I knew what would happen if I told Blackie that yes, Andrew had had a gun, but it was a .38. He'd just say that Andrew, as a returning soldier, might've had more than one.

"Mrs. King, please put this gun back where you keep it. I'm going to tell the police about it. Don't touch it. Please don't fire it—"

"No, no way. I'm afraid of guns."

"Sort of like Tessie?"

"Yeah, just like her, actually." Her sad eyes met mine. "And she told them it was Andrew's?"

"She said they wore her down, ma'am. They just wore her down."

Mama King nodded. She could understand that. "But she was wrong. And if that gun in the picture was the one that hurt my Andrew, then they got to know that Tessie … that she ..." Her gaze went back to the gun case and its content. "You think that what I've told you will help her?"

I rested my hand on the case's surface and ran my fingertips over its nubby surface.

"Yes, ma'am. I think it just might."

But as I left Mama King's, the faint hope that had lightened my heart began to fade. An agile prosecutor would assert that Andrew had a second gun or that Tessie had secured the murder weapon elsewhere. The fact that her fingerprints had not been found on the weapon would mean little to a jury predisposed to find her guilty.

And I did worry that any local jury would be so predisposed.

The main "evidence" against Tessie—her presence at the crime scene and her own self-incriminating request for forgiveness—remained. Then, there was the matter of her formal confession. Those words couldn't be taken back, no matter how hard she tried. That confession would make the job of defending her all that much harder.

And once the news of her confession got out—

What court would be able to seat a jury untainted by prejudice?

I stopped by the station house on my way back to the paper. Blackie was in this time. Through tacit agreement, we didn't refer to our argument, though the taint was still in the air. Me, being me, I pretty much went straight to the point, telling him about my conversation with Macy Dean.

"The upshot of it was that Brandy was scared," I told him. "She was trying to convince Big Earl not to throw his next fight. He'd done it before—welched on a fix—so the mob wanted to make sure he didn't do it again."

"Nice theory. Have you got any proof?"

"I was thinking that that's your job."

"Here we go again."

"Listen, I don't mean to antagonize. It's just that ... Well, I don't understand. You don't seem to want to even look at anybody else. Now, with this mob thing, it's a good lead—"

"I know, Lanie. We've heard the rumors ourselves."

"Well, then."

"Well, then what?"

"Go get some evidence. At least go talk to them." I could hear how I sounded. Snappish. "I'm sorry. "I'm just so ..."

"These people are hard to convict, Lanie. They're professionals. They leave no clues. No witnesses. Nothing."

"So, you won't even try?"

"Lanie," he said, with labored patience. "Sometimes, it takes years to get the evidence needed to indict, then convict these guys. Many times, we fail. I'll admit it. We. Fail. The state was only able to send Madden away for murder because we had witnesses, women who actually help set up Madden's victim. But that was a rarity.

"That's point one. Point two is even simpler: the fact that the mob *might've* had a motive to do the killings doesn't mean they actually did them. And it doesn't change the fact that Tessie King was found there, at the crime scene—"

"I know, I know." I bit my lip, turning the situation over, trying to find something to go for. "The gun—"

"What about it?"

"Andrew's mother said it wasn't his."

His nostrils flared. He realized what I'd done. "You showed her the picture."

"Of course."

"And she said it wasn't his?"

"Yup. She showed me Andrew's gun. It was there, in the house."

He chewed that over, but not for long. "OK, fine, but that doesn't mean he didn't have a second one. Or that Tessie didn't get one somewhere else."

"Did you even test the gun for Andrew's prints?" The look on his face gave me my answer.

"So, all you really have is that she was there, at the crime scene, which she could've stumbled onto, just as she said she did. That's not enough."

He was not to be dissuaded. "She had motive, means, as well as opportunity. To me, that is more than enough."

"Fine," I said, realizing that for now, this topic was a lost cause. "I have one other question."

He leaned back in his chair, ran a hand through his thick black hair and chuckled. "Ah, here, we go."

"What does that mean?"

"It means there's never just one question with you—and you know it. But I don't mind. Let me hear it. What is it?"

I leaned forward and said, "Well, I've been thinking—"

"I'm sure you have—"

"About that caller."

He cleared his throat. "I told you. We don't know his name. He didn't give it."

"I understand that. What I'd like to know is, did he hang up *before* your people could ask him for his name—or *when* they asked for his name?"

"Why are you doing this, Lanie?" He waved a hand. "Oh, don't bother to answer. I know you think you can do my job better than I can, but still."

"I … don't think that." *Not always, anyway.* "It's just a … I just need to know. If you can answer that one for me, I promise to leave it alone."

"Well, the answer is … I don't know."

"You don't know?"

"No."

"Will you look into it?"

A moment of silence, then a sigh.

"All right, all right. I'll do it," he said. "But you know what I think? I think you're making a mountain out of a molehill."

17

B ack in the newsroom, I placed a call to David McKay, a criminal attorney who had himself faced a wrongful murder charge. I had covered his trial. A man of quiet courage and steely resolve, he wasn't one to shy away from a seemingly impossible challenge.

Our conversation was short. David said he'd gotten back into town that morning and had just heard of the case. He listened intently as I gave him an update.

"But the worst is that they got her to confess."

"She *confessed?!*" He sighed. "Well, that changes things. Considerably."

"Meaning you won't take her case?"

"I didn't say that." He paused. "Why did she do it?"

"They got her in a back room."

"Put the thumbscrews on?"

"Hm-hmm—a*nd* s*he*'s convinced herself that it would be best for Mama King, to end it all quickly."

"I see."

I could sense him thinking.

"Well," he said finally. "I'll go talk to her. And see about getting bail. And maybe, just maybe, about getting permission to attend the funeral."

"Doesn't seem likely."

"No, it doesn't."

I told him what Mama King said about the gun. "It will help, won't it?"

"I don't know. If I were the DA, I'd just say that Tessie secured the gun elsewhere. Goodness knows, guns are easy to find these days."

"But that kind? A French—"

"Harlem's full of ex-doughboys, pawning war souvenirs to put food on the table."

"But the prosecutor would have to prove that, wouldn't he? That Andrew had another gun or that she got it at a pawn shop?"

"In theory, yes."

"So much for being innocent until proven guilty." I threw out a suggestion, even though I didn't think it a good one. "What about putting her on the witness stand?"

"I'd be serving her up on a silver platter. She might think she's telling the jury about how much she loved Andrew, but all they'd hear is confirmation of her guilt. That she was jealous and scared of losing him. The prosecutor would have a field day."

He continued, thinking out loud.

"I'll file a motion to have the confession suppressed, kept out of evidence. If we're lucky, I might even get an appointment to see the judge. But I can tell you right now ..."

"You don't think it's going to work."

"Even if it does, even if I succeed in getting that confession kicked, there's no way the jury won't hear about it. You can't keep those things secret. No matter what I say, or the judge instructs, once those good citizens get back in that jury room, once they get back there, they're going to look at each other and say, 'She said she did it, and she didn't say it just once or twice, but over and over again, right there at the crime scene, with all them people listening. And then she even told the police she did it. Now, she wants to take it back, to say she didn't do it. What say you, 'cause I know what I believe.'"

His words painted was a dire picture. Unfortunately, it rang true.

"What are we going to do?" I asked.

He was silent, reflecting. "I don't know," he said, finally, his voice heavy with worry. "I just don't know."

It was time to check back with Nella.

"Got any news for me about the backer who was interested in Andrew?"

"Nope. As far as I can tell, no one in New York City art circles has even heard of an Andrew King, much less been planning to do a showing for him."

I thanked her and hung up, feeling more disappointed than I wanted to admit. Where would Andrew get the idea that someone was backing him? Could Nella be mistaken? She was extremely well-connected, but she didn't know *everyone*. I mean, she couldn't, could she?

Andrew had told Roy about this backer. Surely, he hadn't made him up.

I tapped a pencil on my desktop.

Actually, Andrew had said that someone *told* him that he knew a man who'd be interested in his work. Andrew had actually never met this backer. He'd only been promised an introduction.

The question was, by whom?

That's just what I was pondering when the telephone rang. It was Mama King.

"I just wanted to tell you," she said, "They called right after you left. The police. They said they've done the autopsy. Wanted to know where to …," she hesitated, "to send him. I told them to take him over to Duncan's, over on 135th and Seventh Avenue. You know it?"

I nodded, then remembered that she couldn't see me. "Yes. It's down the street and around the corner from our offices, as a matter-of-fact."

I didn't mention my own painful familiarity with the place, that it was where I'd had them bring Hamp.

Briefly, I wondered about Brandy. The authorities were probably done with her, too. Where was Big Earl having her sent? Most likely Duncan's also.

"I'm going over there now," Mama King said, "I need to make sure everything's ready. He may be there already, for all I know. They're going to prepare him. Duncan's is good, you know."

"Yes, it is, ma'am."

"Maybe, they can repair some of the damage, cover up that … that …"

Her voice broke. She took another moment, then came back strongly.

"They'll have him ready for viewing by tomorrow, at the latest. You're welcome to come by."

"Yes, of course. I'll be sure to do that."

She thanked me and hung up. For a minute, I just sat there, rubbing my forehead, wondering what she had thanked me for. I hadn't done anything to help her or to help Tessie. After a minute of feeling sorry for myself, I straightened up and thought about my next move.

Several seconds later, I got up and headed for Sam's office.

"I need to talk to Big Earl again, but this time without his minder," I said.

Sam looked up at me, over the rims of his new eyeglasses. They made him look sexy.

"So, you still looking to catch that tiger by the tail, huh?"

"He's more like a bull, actually."

"They're both damn dangerous."

"I know, I know. I don't mean to rile him up. Just the opposite, in fact."

Sam frowned. "How's that? You know, that Banks character called here after that last visit you made over to the gym. He called and liked to cuss me out."

"What did you say?"

He shrugged. "Not a thing. I just listened long enough to get the gist of it, then put the phone down and walked away. I came back two minutes later and that was that."

"Well, I guess he got the message loud and clear."

"But Lanie, I don't need that. *You* don't need that. Frankly, I was surprised that he'd even do that. Struck me as a rather ordinary, conservative reaction, considering who he is."

"Are you saying you're disappointed he didn't threaten to rub me out?"

"Heck, for all I know, maybe he did. I wasn't here to listen. All I'm saying is, you got lucky once. Don't count on it happening twice."

"I'm not. Trust me."

Sam inclined his head.

"Sam," I pleaded.

"All right, all right. Big Earl's been keeping a low profile since the killing. Nobody's seen him at the usual hot spots, but …" Sam paused. "There's this little cabaret off 135th and

Fifth. It's in the cellar. Boxers like to hang out there. Otherwise, just regular folk. No swells in there."

"Sounds good."

"It doesn't open till midnight. If he's out and about, you might find him there. And if he *is* there, Banks won't be with him."

"How can you be sure?"

"Well, Banks is white, right?"

"So?"

"The place has a 'no-whites' policy."

Thinking of the whites-only policy of the Cotton Club and other Harlem hot spots, I couldn't believe it.

"You mean, there's actually a place in Harlem where the colored get to tell the whites to keep out?"

"Yup," he said. "There sure is."

"Well, well, well," I said, "imagine that."

18

B ack at my desk, I grabbed my steno pad, reviewed my notes, then reached for the phone.

"Hi, Blackie."

"Lanie."

"I hear the autopsies are done. You got the reports yet?"

"They're right here on my desk."

"Anything you want to share with me?"

"There's nothing in them that you don't know. Confirms everything we suspected."

"Including the caliber of the bullet?"

"The bullet they pulled out of King? It was a .32."

"Sounds like you've got it all tied up, nice and neat."

I tried to sound friendly, like all was normal between us. It wasn't and he knew it. But he tried to pretend, too.

"We're putting it all together for the prosecutor. Assistant District Attorney Bill Ryan will get the case today. Then I'm done with it."

"Well, I still have work to do on it," I said, "because I still have to tighten up, nail down, some details for my stories. You wouldn't mind answering a few questions, would you?"

"Depends."

I clenched my jaw to keep from saying something regrettable and flipped through the pages of my steno pad.

"So, when you talked to folks in the neighborhood, what time did they say they heard the shots?" I checked my notes. *Ten o'clock.*

"Around ten," he said.

All right. I put a checkmark next to that. "Another question."

"Shoot."

"It's about the caller."

"Aw, not him again!"

"Did you check on the business about his name?"

"Lanie, I've been very busy. I—

"Are you sure he said there had been a killing?"

Bless him, he did at least pause to think before answering. "Yes, I think he did."

"Are you sure, Blackie. Really sure?"

"What does it matter?"

"It just does."

He got quiet. His silence lasted for so long that I thought he was going to lose all patience.

"Tell you what," he said, "You're at your office, right? Why don't you come over here and we'll hash this out together?"

* * *

Blackie was waiting for me at the front desk. He asked Wilkins if he'd been the one to take the call on the King-Sullivan killings and the sergeant said he had.

"Did the caller actually say there had been a killing?" Blackie asked.

"Yes, he did," Wilkins said. "I remember it clearly. He was reporting a homicide—and a woman screaming."

"What time did the call come in?" I asked.

Wilkins had this large ledger in front of him and now he

checked it. He turned back a couple of pages, past the incidents that had occurred since the killings. Each page was covered in almost perfect penmanship in blue ink. He ran a mottled finger down the left-hand column until he found what he was looking for.

"It's right here," he tapped the sheet. "The call came in at exactly 10:43 p.m."

"Thank you," I said and turned back to Blackie. "How would he have known there was a shooting if he didn't go inside?"

"Maybe he was standing outside when he heard the shots."

"But everyone puts the shots at around ten o'clock—nearly three-quarters of an hour earlier."

"Maybe, he did go inside—"

"When? When would he have done that?"

He started to answer, but then caught himself. He knew. He knew and he understood. Still, I pressed my point home.

"There's only one way he could've known there was a homicide, and that's if he went inside. Now, are you ready to admit the possibility that someone else—someone other than Tessie—might've been there *before* she got there?"

"Maybe he did go in, but while she was there. How do we know he didn't?"

"She said he didn't. She said no one came, not while she was there."

"And you believe her?"

"Why would she lie about it?"

Blackie wasn't happy, but he was listening. "Let's suppose that everybody's wrong and the shooting happened later than they say it did. Suppose the caller actually did hear the shots, so he knew there'd been a killing that way."

"Shots fired don't mean that somebody's dead. They don't

even mean that somebody's actually been shot. Shots fired means just that, shots fired."

"Yeah." He sounded tired, but he wasn't ready to concede. "I could see why somebody would jump to a conclusion though, especially, if they hear a woman crying."

"I've been thinking about that."

"I bet you have," he muttered.

"If he did hear the shots fired, and Tessie crying, then why didn't he go in and check on her? She could've been the one hurt, the one who was shot."

"Or she could've been the killer, holding the gun, ready to shoot anyone who walked through the door."

"But how would he have known that—without first having walked through the door?"

"Maybe," he said with feigned patience, "he's not like you, Lanie. Maybe, he wouldn't want to take such a chance."

I narrowed my eyes and folded my arms across my chest. "And maybe, just maybe, he's the killer."

There was a long silence.

Blackie worked his jaw. He didn't like the theory, but he didn't mock it. He didn't laugh. He just looked annoyed. But then, bless him, he got to thinking and asked one very good question.

"Why would he have stuck around?"

With that, he had me.

If the shooting had occurred around ten, then why would the killer have hung around, for roughly forty-five long minutes, and then made a call to the police? Even taking into account the time it took for him to do all that damage, it was a long time, a very long time, for him to have hung around.

19

I found the place easy enough, got there around one in the morning.

The first thing to hit me was the intoxicating aroma of reefer and fried chicken. The second was how crowded it was. It was the kind of place that was probably packed a minute after opening.

The place had about six bare wood tables. The menu seemed to mostly consist of chicken dishes, and plates of red beans and rice, from the looks of it. Pigs' feet, too. There was liquor, of course. Lots and lots of bathtub gin.

Like most such places, it wasn't all that bright in there. Under normal circumstances, that and the fact that it was so crowded might've made it hard for me to sight my quarry. But a large good-looking albino sitting at a small bar will stand out in all but the dimmest lights. Of course, the lights behind the bar helped. Thanks to them, Big Earl just about glowed in the dark.

He must've seen me approaching in the mirror behind the bar, because he gave me a nod, then leaned and said something to the man sitting next to him. The fellow slid off the stool and melted into the darkness. I perched on the seat and let Big Earl order me a drink. He raised a finger to signal the bartender, then turned to me.

"What'll you have?"

I glanced at his drink. It would burn like acid going down. "One of those."

"You think you can handle it?"

"Sure, I can. The stronger, the better."

He gave the bartender the order, and ordered another for himself.

"I had a feeling you was gonna show up," he said as the bartender moved away. "Sooner or later, you was gonna come back."

"Like a bad penny?"

"You said it. I didn't." His pale blue eyes measured me. "You still think I did it?"

I started to answer, but the bartender returned with our drinks. I waited till he was gone again.

"Actually," I said, "I don't."

"Why not? You were so damned certain the last time you saw me."

I took a swallow. Coffin varnish. It took all my strength not to gag on it.

"How is it?" he asked, watching me.

"You know damn well how it is. You're drinking the same thing."

He twisted his lips in what passed for a smile. "So, what changed your mind?"

"Things—little things—but big enough to change my mind."

He studied the bottom of his glass. "All right, then. What're you here for?"

I leaned over and whispered in his ear. "To apologize,"

He raised an eyebrow.

"That's right," I said. "I admit that maybe I came on a little too strong before."

"Maybe?"

"Do you accept my apology or not?"

He nodded. "All right, all right. Apology accepted."

"Thank you." I took another sip, held back a choke, and blinked to hold back the tears that welled in my eyes. "Anyway, that's not the only reason I'm here."

"Then what is?"

"To warn you."

His eyes widened. "Warn me?"

"Yeah, but hush. Keep your voice down."

I made a gesture, signaling around us. It was getting noisier and noisier and folks were pressing in on us as they tried to order drinks.

"We need to talk," I said, "but not here."

"Then where?"

* * *

It was easy to pick the lock, to duck under the crime scene tape. I opened the door to Andrew's studio and waved Big Earl in behind me. I turned on my flashlight and headed toward the rear. It was cold back there, with a chill that went to the bone, and the air still held the acrid smell of death.

Big Earl stayed close until I got to the studio and aimed the light at the spot where Andrew and Brandy had lain. Then I heard a low guttural moan. I turned to see the big man frozen at the threshold. His face had turned a dead man's gray.

"Is this … is this where it happened?"

I nodded. The bloodstains were still visible.

He found his feet, approached it slowly, aged suddenly. For a long time, he stood there, staring down at the chalk outlines on the cement floor, outlines united by that dried pool of blood. Finally, he closed his eyes and his powerful hands turned into fists.

"Tell me," he said, "I want to know. Everything. Every detail about what you saw when you got here."

I told him, not everything, but enough. He already knew most of it, from having talked to Blackie and the police. And he'd had to identify Brandy, so he'd actually seen what had been done to her.

They'd released her that day, he said, and as I'd guessed, he'd had her sent to Duncan's for preparation.

"Shot through the mouth," he whispered. "She was *so* pretty, you know? To be shot through the mouth. Her smile, gone. Her life, gone, and for what? Nothing. That's what. For nothing. That bitch shot my baby through the mouth. For nothing. Just 'cause she couldn't keep her man, she—"

"No, no. Tessie didn't do it any more than you did."

"You keep saying that, but—"

"Listen, please. The only difference between you and Tessie is that *you've* got an alibi—but not all that good a one."

"But the police—"

"I know. Your story impressed them, but to me, it don't mean stitches. It could've been bought and paid for."

"I thought you said you—"

"All I'm saying is that once the alibi's out of the way, then you and Tessie are standing on the same shaky ground. You've both got the same motive, same opportunity."

"But you said you don't think I—"

"And I don't."

"Well, *who* then?!"

I tilted my head, narrowed my eyes. "What do you know about Teddy Banks?"

His eyebrow shot up. "Banks?" He shook his head. *"Banks? Nooo!"* He raised his hands and backed away from me. "No!" He was incredulous. "You think *he* did this?"

"What do you know about him?"

"I …" He shrugged. "Nothing. I mean, everything. Everything I need to know."

"You know he's in with Madden, right?"

He didn't respond.

"Course you do," I said. "I'm not gonna make you lie. I'm told you're bad at it, anyway."

He didn't argue. He took a long hard look at where his wife had died.

"Tell me," he said, his voice tight. "Do you think Banks did this?"

I hesitated. "Look … there's rumors—you must've heard them—rumors that you've been throwing fights—"

He opened his mouth to interrupt. I held up a hand to shush him, and went on.

"And that Brandy was trying to get you to stop. That she was pushing you to maybe even go talk to people—people like the Boxing Commission. Now, is that true?"

His jaw worked. He was caught between a rock and a hard place, faced with a choice: to save his own skin by telling a lie or honor his wife by telling the truth.

He walked away, leaned against the wall for support, and buried his face in his hands. Then he slid down to sit on the cold, hard floor.

"I'm done," he murmured. "I'm just so done."

I stood the flashlight on the floor, where it cast a soft, faint glow, like a candle. Then I went and sat down next to him. The atmosphere, believe it or not, was almost church-like. It was the right place for what my mother used to call "the telling," the unburdening of a man's soul.

"We had a dream," he said, "Brandy and me, we had a dream. It was her dream, really. But it sounded mighty fine to me. She was a fantastic cook. Did you know that?"

"No, no, I didn't."

"Man, that little mama could fry her ass off. We was gonna get out of the fight game, and open up a restaurant, in France."

"In Paris?"

"No, Marseille." He paused, as though remembering, and gave a fleeting smile. "Did you know that Brandy danced with Josephine Baker? I think she was better than Baker, myself—but, yeah, she went over to France with Baker to Paris to do that show, that *Revue Negre*. It made Baker famous, but for Brandy ... well, let's just say it didn't work out so good. She left that show, found another and ended up traveling all over the country.

"At some point, she landed in Marseille. Said she loved it there. It had a different vibe. She was gonna stay there, too. Said she never wanted to come back here. But then she got word that her Mama was sick. Had pneumonia. Her family needed her back home. So, home she came. Took the next boat back."

He pursed his lips, then let out a deep sigh. "Her mama died the day before she arrived. Brandy helped with the fun'ral, paid for everything, gave her brother and his family whatever she had. And that included the dough for her ticket back."

He flipped his hands open, as if to say, *And that was that*. "She'd been trying to get back ever since. Told me right upfront when I first met her, that she wasn't gonna be sticking around. Nah, she was gonna be heading back to France."

He leaned his head back and closed his eyes. "Her dream got to be my dream. And we woulda made it, too. We woulda made it."

He opened his eyes, sat up. "I kept telling her, 'Lemme do this one last fight. Just this last one. Don't make no trouble. Don't rock the boat. Just lemme do it and we can get out. But she said, 'No.' Said I shouldn't put myself down for no man, colored or white. Said she was gonna go to the Commission, was even thinking about talking to a reporter, that Sam Delaney guy, writes for your paper.

"She talked to him?" I asked, wondering why Sam hadn't mentioned it.

"No, I don't think so. I think she meant to. I know she said she was thinking about it. But I don't think she even— hell, I don't know."

"So," I said carefully, "did Madden or Big Frenchy know what Brandy was up to?"

His face tightened up, real thoughtful, and he gave a slow nod. "When it first happened, I thought it was them that done it. You know, to shut her up and teach me a lesson. But then I heard about Tessie. That she confessed. That she was … found right here, saying she did it—"

"You heard wrong. I was here. And I heard her. And I'm saying she's no more guilty than you are."

He studied me. "You … you really believe her?"

"Yes, I do. And I'm asking you to trust me. Will you do that?"

He thought about it. "You saying you think the mob did it. That would make it my fault—"

"No, that would make it *their* fault."

"But 'cause of me. 'Cause I agreed to do they dirty work for 'em and then tried to get out. If you right, Miss Lanie, then it's my fault she died. I'm the one they was aiming at when they pulled that trigger. And that means that I'm the one who's gotta make it right."

He started up, as though he meant to do it right then and there. I put out a hand to stop him, grabbed him by the wrist.

"Don't," I said.

"I can't stand here and do nothing."

"You can honor her. You can tell me everything you know

about Banks and his dealings with Madden. You can get out. You can survive—and keep Brandy's memory and her dreams alive."

He said nothing.

"Big Earl?"

He paused. "Miss Lanie, I can't promise you nothing. But I'm gonna ask you to promise me something."

"What?"

"Just one thing: That you'll make 'em pay. I'm trusting you to do it. The right way. 'Cause if you don't, then come hell or high water, I sure 'nuff will."

No doubt about it, he meant every word.

"I'll stay in touch," I said and left it at that.

Dawn was peeping over the horizon by the time I made it home. I climbed the steps to my house, preoccupied with thoughts of what I'd do next.

I put my key in the lock, but before I could turn it, the door swung open and I looked up to find the nozzle of a gun pointing right at my face.

20

A stranger stood in my doorway, a stranger holding a gun on me. My gaze traveled from the tips of his shiny black shoes, to up along his pressed gray pants, his black coat, wide set shoulders, square cut jaw, to the dead black eyes under his fedora.

He stepped back, opening the door, and gestured for me to enter.

I could've tried to cut and run. For a split second, I certainly considered it. But it hit me that if the mob wanted to me dead, then I would've been dead already. They would've cut me down right out on the street, in the open for the world to see. Something like that, it makes an impression, sends a message, and they just loved to do both.

Of course, there was no guarantee they wouldn't take a certain sadistic joy in cutting me down inside my own home. There's never a guarantee as to which way the wind blows when it comes to something like that.

Still, I thought the chances were in my favor. So, I followed him. I followed that thug as he presumed to lead me into *my own house*—the house my Hamp had bought for me.

The foreign smell of bitter tobacco poisoned the air. I walked into the parlor to find Frenchy DeMange sitting in Hamp's armchair before the fireplace, smoking a cigar. He inhabited it like a king, as though he owned the place. Another henchman stood, with folded hands, to his right. The man who'd opened my own door to me took up his place at DeMange's left.

DeMange waved for me to take a seat, treating me like a guest.

"No, thanks," I said. "I prefer to stand."

"Come on," he said, gesturing with the cigar. "I don't want to hurt you. Sit down. I just want to have a chat."

I glanced at the two mugs on either side of him. They had the same mien, and appeared to be not too bright, but for all that, all the more lethal.

DeMange said, "They make you nervous?"

I said, "What do you think?"

He snapped his fingers and pointed to the door. They each gave me an icy look, then silently filed out, closing the door after them.

He gestured to the other chair. "Now, would you sit down?"

I shouldered out of my fur coat, draped it over my hands and eased down into the chair, clutching my purse.

"What do you want?"

"You been snooping around. Getting on the wrong people's nerves. You know that, right?"

"I repeat. What do you want?"

His heavy jaw went slack in surprise. No doubt, he wasn't used to being spoken to like that, certainly not by a woman and a colored one at that.

"You're a mouthy little bitch, aren't you?"

"And you're in my home, without an invitation."

He took the cigar from his mouth. "I could have my men here show you some manners."

"Try it and you'll be dead before you know it."

I showed him the muzzle of the .25 caliber tucked inside my hand.

"What the fuck! Didn't that idiot frisk you?"

"Obviously, he didn't."

"Put it away. You cain't hurt nobody with that peashooter."

"I can hurt you a'plenty. You've got a small brain, but a big head. At this distance, I won't miss."

"My men—"

"May kill me dead, but they won't make it in time to save you."

His cold eyes narrowed. He sank back in the chair. "You know, I like you. You got guts."

"Tell me something I haven't heard before."

"All right. I'll make you a deal. I tell you the truth about the Brandy-Big Earl situation and you lay off."

I studied his heavy-jawed mug and didn't find a thing to like about it, much less trust.

"If you want to talk to me about Brandy and Big Earl, then I'm willing to listen. But I don't make promises I can't keep."

"You don't get it, do you? I'm trying to help you, here. Maybe, even save your life."

"So, you're here to warn me?"

"To deliver a message."

I leaned back in my chair. "I'm listening."

"As you well know, Brandy was running around shooting her mouth off. She was talking crazy, threatening to talk to the Boxing Commission about fight fixing and what not." He waved his cigar. "It was nonsense, of course. Utter nonsense. It was all in her head."

"But there was a chance that someone might've believed her, right?"

He surprised me by agreeing. "Right."

"So, you guys had her killed, right?"

"No. Of course, not. Look," he put up his hands. "This has all been a big misunderstanding. Macy Dean shoulda never opened her mouth. She shouldna been spreading rumors like that. We had to have a little heart-to-heart with her—and now she knows not to do it again."

"You've hurt her."

"Macy? No. She ain't worth the trouble. We gave her a choice and she made a smart decision. That's all. Let's just say, she won't be dancing for us no more—and not for nobody else in New York, neither—not now, not ever."

That was unfortunate. I held myself to blame for that. She'd been brave to talk to me. My approaching her had exposed her and could've cost her her life.

He gave a little smile. It was about as warm as an alligator's.

"Returning to the subject of Brandy. Now, I won't pretend there wasn't some discussion among the boys about how to handle her, but ultimately, we decided not to do nothing … well, nothing permanent, anyways—"

I didn't quite believe that. "Why?"

He gave a vague gesture and a shrug. "Just because. We … well, we decided it wouldn't be the most prudent thing to do."

He glanced at me with those lizard eyes to see if I believed him. I didn't and I didn't try to hide it.

"Go on," I said.

"This is the thing." He leaned toward me, his face alight with a devilish glow, and dropped his voice to a confidential low. "Teddy Banks, you know, her husband's manager? He said he'd take care of it."

"He *did?*"

"Told us that if we left the matter in his hands, he'd handle it. Said he'd make sure she never said another word." He grinned. "And guess what? He did."

"And why would he agree to do that?"

"Ain't it obvious?"

"No."

"Why, to get in good with us, of course."

He gestured expansively, then settled back in the chair, his slit eyes, speculative and watchful. I returned his gaze, also thoughtful. The fire behind the grate crackled and a log fell into place.

"I'm surprised you'd turn on your buddy and give me all this information."

"Oh, I'm not turning on nobody," he said amiably. "You try to print what I just told you and we'll sue you and your paper for defamation of character."

He adjusted his silk tie. "What was said here was off the record. If you try and make it any different, well … we'll see who comes out ahead."

He smiled. "But what I can add is this—and it *is* on the record. Banks ain't my buddy. You get me? Banks stinks to high heaven. We don't trust him as far as we can throw him. Now, *that,* little sister, that is something you *can* print."

21

I overslept the next morning and was late getting to the newsroom, not that it mattered. One of the great things about my job was that I didn't have to punch a clock. I could come and go as I pleased, so long as I got my stories and filed them on time.

Blackie had left a message for me. When I called him back, he got straight to the point.

"I need you to back off, Lanie."

"Back off from what?" I asked, even though I had a feeling I knew the answer.

"Drop the Teddy Banks angle, the mob, the whole thing."

"Why?"

"Because."

"Because isn't good enough."

There was a long silence. Then he cleared his throat.

"Just trust me on this one. The Banks angle won't get you anywhere."

"I've heard different."

I told him about my visit from the mob.

"Lanie, I know what it sounds like. But we both know you

can't trust those thugs. Has it occurred to you that maybe there's a reason why they fed you this cock and bull story about Banks?"

"Of course, it occurred to me. What I want to know is why you're confident that it *is* a story. You don't want to tell me why?"

"No."

For a minute there, a long minute, I actually found myself wondering whether Blackie was on the take. I told myself it wasn't possible. Lying to a suspect, that was one thing. But bribery, corruption? That was another. One of the reasons the mob operated with such impunity was its ability to corrupt good men, and the inability of others to recognize it when it was happening.

"Are you involved in this?"

I could feel his shock. It reverberated down the line.

He started to speak, then held back. "Lanie," he said finally, his voice tight. "You know me better 'n that."

I hoped I did. "Then why?"

"I'm asking you. Please. Drop it. Go no further. It's the wrong road you'd be taken. Trust me on it."

I drew a deep breath. "The thing is, I do trust you. Even after what you pulled with Tessie, I trust you. Generally speaking, that is—but not on this. Maybe it's *because* of what you pulled with Tessie. I don't know. What I do know is that, in my heart of hearts, I want to trust you, but my head says, 'Don't.'"

"Lanie, I—"

"There's more to Banks than meets the eye. He's a liar, and maybe a killer. I'll be writing my story today and Banks is going to be in it."

* * *

I rolled a fresh sheet of paper into my typewriter, then laid out my notes and glanced over them. I had a pretty good idea of how to start the article and where to go with it.

Actually, there would be more than one article. I would …

I had just raised my hands over the keyboard, my fingers poised to type, when the phone rang.

It was Blackie. The conversation that followed wasn't a conversation at all.

"Lanie, we need to see you," he said.

"If it's about our earlier—"

"Be over here in five minutes." He paused, then dropped his voice, his tone softer. "Come. Otherwise, they'll make me come and get you. And that," he sighed, "that wouldn't be good for either of us."

Then I heard the click of the line as he hung up.

He'd never spoken to me like that. Many times, I knew I overstepped the boundaries of the relationship between whites and blacks, cops and civilians. Many times, I wondered by Blackie tolerated it. He was just different. So, whatever had caused him to use that tone with me, it was serious.

I gathered up my things and went.

* * *

Wilkins picked up the phone as soon as I walked in. Seconds later, Blackie came out to get me.

"What's going on?" I asked.

"Follow me."

He escorted me to an office in the rear. It didn't appear to be normally used. The desk was empty and there were no books or files to be seen anywhere. However, the room itself was not empty.

Teddy Banks perched on the edge of the desk, hands crossed almost contemplatively in his lap. He stood when we entered the room.

Something was different about him. His clothes, for one

thing. They were somber and conservative instead of his usual flamboyant and attention-getting. But there was something else, something about the man himself.

Blackie closed the door, shutting us in together.

"Mrs. Price," he said with unusual formality, walking around me to stand next to Banks and fold his arms across his chest. "I'd like to introduce you to Special Agent Kent—Robert Kent—from the Bureau of Prohibition."

"What?" I said.

Banks stepped forward, extending a hand. "Mrs. Price," he said. "I'm with the Bureau."

I felt faint. "You … you're a federal agent?"

"Here," Blackie said, putting a gentle hand on the base of my back. "Why don't you take a seat?"

I stared at him. "This is true?"

"Yes. Now, sit down." He pulled out a chair and gently, but firmly pushed me down into it.

Teddy Banks—or rather Special Agent Kent—said, "Mrs. Price, please listen carefully. Nothing that is said within this room may be repeated, or printed. Do you understand?"

I nodded, still in a daze. They talked. I listened. There's no need to go into detail—there weren't that many of them, actually. It really all boiled down to one thing: Banks, rather Kent, was an undercover agent. His role as Big Earl's agent enabled him to get close to Madden and his operation at the Cotton Club. And his authority as an agent explained his knowledge about details of the King-Sullivan crime, knowledge that had first made me suspect him.

"Does Big Earl know about this?" I asked.

"No."

"You've fixed fights for him?"

"As part of my role, I've had to. Yes."

"But the part about Andrew and Brandy …"

"It's true, what Big Frenchy said. I did offer to 'take care of her.'"

"But you supposedly did it to protect her?"

"No supposing about it," Banks said.

"So, you see," Blackie said. "The man you know as Banks, he couldn't have—"

"Yes, I understand." I felt as though I'd been ambushed. I turned to Banks–*Kent*. His new name—or rather *real* name—was going to take some getting used to. "But how do you know, absolutely know for certain, that Big Frenchy didn't go around you and—"

"Have someone else do it?" Banks finished.

I nodded.

"I'm pretty confident I would've heard about it. And ..." he paused, "well, let's just say they would've done it differently."

I wanted to ask Banks what he meant by that, but Blackie's next words made it clear that for him the meeting was over.

"So, now, you understand?" Blackie said to me. "There's no reason to investigate him—or write about him."

"I can think of one very good reason," I said.

They both looked at me, Blackie with annoyance, Banks with a raised eyebrow.

"Go on," Banks said, "tell me why."

"The mob doesn't trust you. Big Frenchy was very clear about that. After what he told me, they'll trust you even less if I don't write about you."

"Hmph." Banks rubbed his chin, and threw Blackie a glance, as if to ask him what he thought.

"She's got a point," Blackie said.

Banks considered it some more, then nodded. "I'm afraid she does."

I stood, ready to leave their charming company.

"So, thank you for this little meeting," I said, "and the trust you've shown me, Agent Kent, by revealing yourself. Trust me, I'll pay you back by slinging as much mud your way as possible."

Banks gave a wry smile. "Why, thank you."

"And that goes for you, too," I told Blackie. "I wouldn't want you to feel left out."

"Of course, not," he said. "Heaven forbid."

Banks offered me his hand once more and this time I took it.

Blackie escorted me back out and stood with me a few minutes at the front desk.

"Lanie," he said. "This thing with Special Agent Kent, all joking aside, I do hope you realize that it places the spotlight back on Tessie King. There's no getting around it. She's—"

"She's innocent. I still believe that."

"But Lanie, there's no one else. Not Big Earl, not Teddy Banks, not the mob at large."

"We'll see," was all I could muster. "We'll just have to see."

It was a brave front and he saw through it. He was gracious enough to not say more, and I walked out, feeling thoroughly deflated.

If I didn't come up with something and soon, then Mama King would lose not only her son, but a daughter-in-law she'd come to depend on. Tessie would go to prison for a crime she hadn't committed.

And a killer would go free.

22

I sat at my desk, cogitating. The meeting with Blackie, learning the truth about Banks, it took the wind out of my sails. No lie.

At times like this, I've found that the best thing to do is to take a step back, go back to the beginning, reconsider everything. So, that's what I was doing. Sitting at my desk, hands clasped and eyes closed, cogitating.

The sounds of the newsroom faded. The clickety-clack of typewriters, the whoosh of the pneumatic tubes, the shrill ringing of telephones and the chatter of my colleagues' voices—it all sank away. All that remained was my inner voice and inner space for me to listen to it.

I started with the nude photographs.

Those pictures had cemented the assumption that jealousy was the motive, that Andrew died because he took the wrong pictures of the wrong woman. The only two people known to have that kind of motive were Tessie and Big Earl, so it made sense to focus on them.

Once I had moved on to suspect the mob's hand in the

killings, I'd set aside any thoughts about their possible guilt. But maybe I needed to reconsider.

Tessie and Big Earl. Was I wrong about them? Had one of them done it, after all?

It just didn't feel right.

If Tessie or Big Earl had known about the pictures and pulled the trigger because of what they implied, would they have left those pictures for the cops to find?

It didn't seem likely. Any decent defense attorney could argue that in this instance the very evidence seen as suggesting guilt could also be viewed as suggesting innocence.

I took a deep breath and let it out slowly.

Those photographs. Those photographs.

We'd been so focused on them, we'd let it dominate our thinking. Maybe the killer hadn't even known about them or had simply overlooked them. Or—

My breath caught at a sudden sliver of insight.

Or maybe, just maybe, he hadn't cared about them.

Had he sought something else entirely?

I toyed with that idea for a while.

It made sense, especially in light of what Macy Dean had told me. It fit the suspicion that Madden had ordered the killing to silence and punish Brandy and bring Big Earl back in line. And that Andrew was simply in the wrong place at the wrong time.

I paused at that part.

Wrong place, wrong time.

It was *his* studio, *his* place of business. If the mob was primarily interested in Brandy and Big Earl, then why strike there? Why not catch Brandy alone? Or was there a reason for killing Andrew, too?

I frowned, sank lower in my chair and massaged the muscle between my eyes.

Could Andrew have taken a photo or hidden something in that backroom that would've helped Brandy but in the end got them both killed?

That darkroom and those destroyed photographic plates.

The time it had taken to go through them and smash them. The confidence the killer must've had that no one would hear him.

Why would he have stuck around? Blackie had asked.

Because he was looking for something.

And that something was not the photos of Brandy.

I sat up, eyes narrowed, returning to an earlier thought. Maybe, the killer had indeed known about those pictures. And maybe he had good reason for leaving them there.

He wanted them found because they would mislead investigators, distract them from the true purpose of the killings and the destruction he'd left behind.

I had to get back inside that studio. The answer was there.

But first, I had somewhere else to go.

* * *

The Duncan Brothers Funeral Home was well-known and trusted. It had received and taken care of many of Harlem's most cherished, most prominent men and women. When Barron Wilkins, the owner of Barron's Exclusive Club, was shot and killed by a thief he'd once tried to help, it was Duncan's that took care of Wilkins's remains.

It was, as a matter of fact, just around the corner from my office, on the ground floor of a four-story apartment building. The moment I stepped inside its entry, I became enveloped in the thick fragrance of flowers and the hushed heavy silence so particular to funeral parlors and chapels.

Mama King was there when I arrived, as was Mrs. Dill and other church ladies I recognized from attending their social events. Mama King came over when she saw me.

"You came," she said, her face lighting up with a gentle, if sorrowful smile.

"Yes."

"I'm glad you made it today," she said. "Today and tomorrow, they just for friends of the family. The day of the funeral, I guess the whole world will be coming in."

It was clear that she would've preferred to keep the funeral private. I didn't take this as any sign of resentment toward the public in general, and most especially not Andrew's fans in particular, but just the wishes of a mother in mourning. Together, we walked over to the bier.

"Mr. Van Der Zee will be here later this evening," she said, "to take Andrew's picture. He's offered to do that."

"That was awfully kind of him. Will he do one of his collages, one of his special photos for you?"

"I think so."

Van Der Zee was known for his technique of superimposing photos of lost loved ones on portraits of those left behind. The results often gave great comfort to the living.

"Did you have him take a photo of your husband when he died?" she asked.

"No, I didn't." To tell the truth, at the time it didn't even occur to me. I doubt I would've done it if it had. "I already had the picture of Hamp that I still treasure the most. And your son took it."

She smiled with trembling lips at that, bowed her head and blinked rapidly. Mrs. Dill came over.

"Mama King, are you all right?" She wrapped an arm around the elderly woman's thin waist—and threw me a disapproving glance over her shoulder.

"I think I need to sit down for a minute," Mama King said.

"Oh, I'm sorry," I said. "Can I help?"

"No, we'll be fine." Mrs. Dill waved me away.

"You stay and take your time," Mama King said, and then let Mrs. Dill walk her away. The old woman seemed much weaker and frailer than she had even the day before. The murder of her only child—and no doubt, the jailing of his wife for the murder—were sapping the life out of her.

I turned back to Andrew. The undertaker had done an amazing job in restoring Andrew's appearance. But he hadn't been able to wipe away the trauma of Andrew's last moments. The terror and maybe even anger Andrew must've felt were deeply etched into his face.

Gazing down into his coffin, I thought of Brandy, and wondered. *Did they even know why they were being attacked? Did they have any idea of the killer's motive?*

It seemed logical to assume they would have, but standing there, thinking about it, I wasn't so sure. Nothing in anything Tessie had said so far indicated that Andrew had been receiving threats or sensed he was in any danger.

I pictured the studio's front door. He'd kept it locked when he worked there at night. Would he have opened it to strangers, or only to someone he knew? It had shown no sign of violent entry. So, he knew his killer.

Not at first.

But by the end, he knew—they both did. Only, by then, it was too late.

* * *

Late that night, I returned to King's Studio and glanced around. No one was looking. Across the street, the newsstand was closed. I slipped down the stairs to the entrance and went to work picking the lock.

Once inside, I depended on the muted light from the street lamps to make my way to the back, to where the bodies were found. Once there, I felt for a wall switch and flicked it on. I glanced at the chalk outlines that marked the floor, then hurried past them and on to the room Andrew had used as an office.

The place was a mess. I stood there, surveying the damage and feeling suddenly overwhelmed. What could I possibly hope to find? Would I even recognize it if I found it?

I took a deep breath and told myself to think logically. I was looking for something left behind, and/or something taken. The problem, of course, was that I wasn't familiar with the contents of Andrew's office. I might not notice what was missing or what ought not to be there.

I decided it would help to impose some order on the place. But first, it might make sense to just stand here and observe. Perhaps there was some underlying order in the disorder, one that would be destroyed once I got to work.

There was.

The killer had concentrated most of his—or her—energy on the shelves holding the books and the papers. Yes, some of the equipment had been knocked to the floor, but most of it was still in place. Maybe, the killer had left them there because they were heavy—or maybe it was because the focus was elsewhere.

Time to get to work. I cast a rueful glance at the cast-iron stove in the corner. The office was chilly. It would've been nice to have had some heat.

For a good hour, I sifted through the detritus of Andrew's career, separating the papers from the books, creating small stacks of each, and setting the equipment to one side. Finally, I sank to the floor and surveyed the results. The papers didn't seem to add up to much. It was mostly correspondence, invoices and receipts. Every now and then, I turned up a news article or two. As for the books, they turned out to be photo collections. In the end, they're what caught my eye.

There were several of them and when I put them

together, I saw that they were part of a series. He'd labeled each one with a month and year, starting with January 1925.

I picked out one at random and flipped through it. It contained pictures of West 122nd Street and Seventh Avenue, the intersection just south of the studio. The shots had been taken from the northeast corner. There was the church on the southwest, the Fish 'n' Fry on the southeast, and a stream of vehicles and pedestrians flowing up and down the avenue in between. Two pictures per day taken from the same spot: one in the morning when people were rushing to work; one in the evening, when they were dragging themselves home. The individual pictures said little, but they made powerful testimony as a whole.

I closed the collection book and sat with it on my lap, gazing at the stack of albums. I thought about all the work, the dedication, that had gone into making them. From January of '25 onward, Andrew had faithfully created the photos for each and compiled them one by one. My gaze came to rest on the last album.

It was for last month. Hmm.

Where was the album for this month, the month of September?

I glanced around. Had I missed it? Or was it in the darkroom, perhaps, for Andrew to add photos to it? Or to show it to the prospective sponsor?

I searched around for several minutes, then got up and went to the darkroom, where I searched some more. The darkroom, with shattered glass everywhere, was ghostly.

I didn't see the photo collection for September anywhere. Perhaps there was nothing odd about its absence.

But perhaps, there was.

23

Unable to sleep, I woke earlier than usual the next morning, got ready, stepped outside and froze. The temperature had taken a nosedive overnight. The wind kissed my ankles and I nearly yelped.

I headed back inside and hurried upstairs to my bedroom. I shrugged out of my coat, put on a wool sweater, then paused and grabbed a second one. I went to my dresser and took out a couple of pairs of thick socks, then used the sweater to roll it all up in a neat bundle together.

Minutes later, I was motoring downtown to the Harlem Courthouse, making good time.

The jailer checked the bundle then led me to Tessie's cell. She looked even thinner than before and her skin had taken on a flat gray. She was turning into a ghost before my eyes.

"Miss Lanie?" she blinked at me sleepily. "What are you doing here so early?"

I looked at her in that thin jail uniform and gave a little shiver. She didn't seem to be affected by the cold—maybe she was too far gone to notice it—but I did.

"Here," I said, handing her the sweater and two pairs of socks.

Her eyes brightened at the sight of them. "Oh, thank you. But you didn't have to—"

"Don't thank me. Just please put them on. Just looking at you makes me feel chilly."

She rewarded me with a thin smile, fingered the sweater and buried her nose in it. "Hmm. It smells good, too."

"Chanel No. 5, dahling. Chanel No. 5! Only the best for you!"

There! A real smile. It was good to see.

"Tessie," I said more soberly, "I need you to tell me something. Where did Andrew archive his professional prints?"

"His prints?" She repeated, slipping an arm into one sleeve.

"Yes, prints of photos. They all seemed to have been taken from the same corner—"

"Oh, those. He kept them in books—big albums—in his studio. Why?"

"He kept all of them there?"

She nodded, buttoning the sweater.

"He didn't bring any of them home?"

"No. Why?"

I told her.

"That album should be there," she said. "It was definitely there that morning. I put it together myself. You see, it was part of a special project Andrew was doing. He wanted to document the changes in the neighborhood."

"This project. I've heard of it. Tell me more."

She was happy to do so.

"Well, Andrew had this idea and, like all good ideas, it was elegant and simple. He used to set up his camera, every day. Same spot. Same time. Twice a day. Every day. We even had a name for the exhibit: *A Living History: The Changing Faces of Lenox.*"

Her face suffused with unexpected joy. It changed her and in a way revealed her. It dawned on me that behind those large spectacles, Tessie was actually quite pretty. I wondered if the glasses were as much for hiding behind as for seeing through. Some of us, we hide our beauty. Because we find it safer to be invisible. A part of me wondered if Tessie wasn't like that.

"He was special," she was saying. "He had a way..." she paused, "a way of making regular people, everyday people, feel important. Oh, he liked working with celebrities, but he enjoyed the regular folk even more. People who'd been told they didn't matter since the day they were born—he liked to show them that that was wrong, that they were special, too. It just took somebody to see it is all. That's what he used to tell me. That it just took somebody to see it—and to make them believe it.

"And my part," she said with a hint of pride, "was to put those pictures he took in an album, to keep them in order, make sure they were safe." She paused, remembering, then looked back at me. "So yes, I'm sure, that album was there that day." She tilted her head. "Are you sure it's gone?"

"I searched everywhere for it."

"But why would anyone take it?"

A very good question.

* * *

Riverside Park, in general, and that stretch of the embankment along the Hudson River, in particular, was rather deserted that day. Icy gusts of wind whipped fallen leaves into swirling mini-tornadoes. Those dead leaves were the liveliest, most colorful things out there. Everything else was shades of gray.

This was September, but it felt like December.

Apparently, Mother Nature was in a hurry and had decided to skip a couple of months along the way.

I tugged my cloche hat a little more firmly down on my head and hurried along, my shoes clicking on the pavement. I was five minutes late.

He was already there, just that one lone soul, leaning on the stone wall, smoking a cigarette and gazing out over the river, to the distant Jersey shore. He was back in costume, wearing the natty threads of an underworld character.

"So, you came to apologize?" he asked.

"In your dreams," I said, coming to stand next to him, catching my breath against the unseasonable cold. It was a miserable day, very New York, very grim. Very hard.

He glanced at me, a hint of amusement in his eyes.

"Why else would you want to see me, if not to apologize?"

"You said something, before, at the police station. I wanted to follow up on it."

He inclined his head, curious. Up close, he presented an odd contrast. To the eye, he was Teddy Banks, a rascally low-life weasel. To the ear, he was a well-educated, well-spoken agent. The only shared characteristic was the toughness. That remained whether he was Banks or Kent.

"So, tell me," he said. "Why the meet?"

"You said the mob would've 'done it differently.' What did you mean by that?"

He didn't answer at first. He seemed more interested in the movements of a tiny tugboat making its way upriver than in answering my question. When he did answer, it was with a question.

"What's bothering you? From what Blackie tells me, and from what I've seen, you've got good instincts. What're they telling you?"

I took a minute to think about it.

"It's the gunshots," I finally said. "One to his eye and one to her mouth. They practically screamed mob. I'm beginning to wonder if it wasn't all a bit too-too."

"Too obvious?"

"Exactly."

Kent drew on his cigarette, then blew out a long stream of smoke.

"I'm not going to agree or disagree. But what I will say is this. What I know of the crime doesn't fit the picture of Tessie King, not according to what we have on file about her—"

"You have a file on Tessie?"

He smiled opaquely. "We have a 'file' on just about everybody. The Bureau's very concerned about what's going on in Harlem these days. All these efforts by Commie's to recruit people."

"But Tessie? And, by extension, I suppose that includes Andrew?"

"She's a writer, with a very strong voice. Let's just leave it at that." He tapped his cigarette, watched the ash float away. "Back to your case. Here, you have a woman who's supposedly terrified of guns. But she's accused of having shot her husband and his lover in a fit of rage. It's not impossible, of course, but it's not likely. This killing, it was precise and cold. I think whoever did it is familiar with guns, very familiar. He—or *she*—is used to pulling that trigger, maybe even doing it with pleasure."

"But that would take us back to the mob, wouldn't it?"

"Would it?" He raised an eyebrow.

His expression told me he was enjoying himself. Mine told him I wasn't.

"Look," he said, "They were planning on doing Brandy, for sure, but not Andrew. They had zero interest in him. If they had decided to take her out, they would've done it clean.

They would've left her somewhere anonymous, maybe in an empty lot or outside with the trash. Not in the back of a studio, next to some community hero."

He took one last draw on his cigarette, then flicked the butt away.

"Did you tell Blackie you don't think Tessie did it?" I asked.

"This is a local case. The feds are hands' off."

"Then why did you agree to talk to me?"

The edges of his lips twitched a hint of amusement. "Let's just say I'm doing Blackie a favor."

"He wanted you to talk to me?"

"I think he was hoping I could convince you that (a) she's guilty and (b) to stay out of it."

"Hmph! Fat chance of that!"

"Yup," he chuckled. "That's what I said."

24

There's something about Riverside Drive, about standing there, watching that river, that's always made me feel like I've left the city. That's the good of it and the bad of it, I guess. After all, who doesn't need a break sometimes, from New York City?

So, I stood there for a while after Kent left, stood there thinking. About all the wrong turns I'd taken in this case. And how I still didn't have any good news to give Mama King.

Then I told myself that it was time to stop feeling sorry for myself. It was time to get back to business and that meant heading back across town, where a certain attorney was no doubt checking his watch and wondering what he'd gotten himself into.

* * *

As a matter-of-fact, David McKay was indeed looking at his watch when I walked in the Fish n' Fry. He'd taken a table by the window, so you would've thought he'd have seen me first. But he had his nose in a thick folder of impressive-looking papers.

I slid onto the seat across from him, gestured to the folder, and said, "Anything interesting?"

"Maybe, but I'll save it for another day."

"Sorry, I'm late."

"It's OK. Knowing you, I'm sure you had good reason."

"Well, thank you."

"Just don't let it happen again."

He signaled Darleen. She happened to be at the end of the counter near our table. She grabbed up the pitcher of coffee, as well as a cup and saucer and brought them over, a menu tucked under one arm. David already had his coffee. So, she refreshed his after pouring mine.

"You both want the usual? Or do you want to be bold and try something different?"

Darleen knew every single one of her regular customers' orders. It's what made going to her diner so special. She made you feel like you were visiting the home of a gruff, but loving relative.

"The usual," David and I said at the same time.

Darleen gave a grunt and shuffled away.

"So," David turned to me, "what do you want to hear first? The good news or the bad?"

I shrugged. "Six of one, half dozen of the other."

"OK, then. They've moved up Tessie's prelim date. It's in three days."

"Why?" I frowned.

"Judge said he wanted to get the case done. This is bad."

"How bad?"

"Very bad. You never want a prelim when emotions are running high."

"What're we going to do?"

"Push for a delay. I don't doubt she'll be bound over and the chances of it being a fair trial are slim to none. Not right now. There's a mountain of circumstantial evidence and it's all against her."

"What about the funeral? She desperately wants to attend Andrew's funeral."

"It's not likely, but I'll try. The medical examiner's already released the body."

"I know. The funeral is in two days."

He took that with a grim nod. "Then I'd better get going. I've only got a couple of hours, at most, to convince the judge to let Tessie out."

He didn't say it, but I knew what he was thinking: two days till the funeral; three till the prelim. The clock was ticking.

"By the way, what's the good news?" I asked. Then, it hit me. "That *was* the good news? That they've moved up the prelim?"

"Yup. She won't have to wait for long."

* * *

In leaving the diner, I noticed Thelma Lee. She stood on the corner of 122nd Street and Lenox Avenue. She stopped a teenage boy and held out the sketch that bore her daughter's penciled likeness. The boy shook his head and moved on.

Across the street, the newsdealer also watched her. I crossed the street to his stand. Jackson gave me a nod, then returned his gaze to Cana's mother, his brows furrowed.

"God help her. She's a good woman. I hope she finds that child soon."

"You know her, the little girl?"

"I seen her around. Cute little thing. Sweet as an angel."

I leaned on the display of newspapers, feeling their slightly damp weight give beneath me, and dropped my voice down low, real confidential-like.

"Listen, I heard that Andrew was expecting somebody to

come by—a white guy who was going to put his work up in an exhibit."

His eyebrows went up. "Is that so?"

"So I heard."

"And you say, he was s'posed to come by and see Andrew?"

"Hm-hmm."

He picked up the baseball, started tossing it from hand to hand, as he thought about it.

"Well, now that you mention it ..."

"Yes?"

"There *was* this one guy." Jackson frowned and scrunched up his mouth with thought. "A little white guy. White hair, white suit. Even had a cane and spats. Like he thought he was a plantation owner."

"What time was this?"

"Maybe, around half-past nine." He scratched his brow. "You can't be thinking he had something to do with it?"

"Don't know, but I'm going to find out." I straightened up. "Did you tell the cops this?"

"Nah," he shrugged. "It just didn't seem important at the time."

I can see why he thought that. But he was wrong. With that short description, Jackson had broken the case.

If only I'd realized it at the time.

25

I walked down to the corner to talk to Thelma Lee. She looked bone-tired.

"How's your search going?" I asked.

She shook her head. "Ain't nobody seen nothing."

I glanced down at the sketch she held. It was worn and smudged.

"How long have you been looking?"

"Five days. Since Saturday."

"And nobody's seen nothing?"

"If they did, they ain't saying."

"You've been to the police?"

She gave a little snort. "They don't care nothing 'bout our children. Won't even take a report."

"You went to the 135th Street station?"

"Why? You know the cops there?"

"One or two of them. Who'd you talk to?" She gave me a name. "You know him?'

"I may have seen him around."

"He's at the front desk. Told me they got more important things to do than run down some snotty-nosed kids. No, they don't care. Our kids is disappearing off the streets, and the cops don't care."

"*Kids?*"

"My Cana, she ain't the first one to go missing from 'round here, and I'm thinking she won't be the last. There was them two little girls back in February. One of them, they found her, shot dead. The other girl, they ain't never found her.

"Then there was that other child, just this past summer. All they found of her was her bike, leaned up 'gainst a tree over there in Mount Morris Park. And it wasn't even the cops that found that, just somebody walking by."

I listened, surprised and ashamed. I hadn't heard of any of these cases. I generally knew what everyone was working on at the paper and I made a habit of reading our paper from cover to cover every week. Yet, I knew nothing about them. Had heard nothing about them.

"And the cops won't look," she was saying. "They won't even try. They keep saying our kids is running away, but we know that ain't so. They was taken. Somebody out there is taking our kids and the police won't do nothing 'bout it."

She narrowed her eyes. "How come you know the police?"

"I'm a reporter. Write for the *Harlem Chronicle.*"

"Oh. So, that's why I been seeing you down here. You been going 'round, talking to a lot of people. You down here cause of what happened to that photographer and the dancer, right?"

"You see anything?"

She shook her head and eyed me, a faint hope lighting her eyes. "You think you could write a story on my Cana?"

In truth, I was thinking of doing just that, but I don't like making promises I might not be able to keep, so I gave a noncommittal shrug and said, "Maybe."

The hope in her eyes died quick.

"That's okay," she said, with only a pinch of bitterness and a dash of resignation. "I knew you weren't gonna do nothing. I don't know what I was thinking. High-siddity people like you …" She gave a little shrug and raised her chin with dignity. "But thank you for listening."

"Listen, I—"

She raised a hand. "Like I said, it's OK. Now, s'cuse me, but I gotta go back to looking for my baby."

26

When I returned to the newsroom, the first thing I did was contact Nella.

"I'm still looking," she said.

I gave her the description Jackson provided.

"Nope," she said. "That doesn't sound like anyone I know, and I know *everyone*. Look," she added, "I've been thinking this over, and I have to say, I'm finding it all rather strange. Surely, if someone had been interested, he would've stepped forward the minute Andrew died. I mean, it sounds crass, but from a purely business point of view, an artist's work gains in value the moment he dies. So, if this guy is out there—if he *really* exists, and he's legitimate—then he should've been making a beeline to the studio door—or to whoever's in charge of Andrew's estate. The people I know, they've would've been positively making a pest of themselves, trying to sew up the rights. Have you talked to the wife? Asked her whether she's heard from anyone like that?"

"No, but I will."

"Well, if she says she hasn't, then you truly have to ask if he even exists," Nella said. "Because, for my money, he doesn't."

Nella had a point.

I didn't have time to go down to the jail to see Tessie, so I picked up the phone and called the jail instead. I had little hope that the man in charge would agree to bring her to the phone, but he did. Of course, it might've helped that I hedged my bet by saying that I was with her attorney, which was not entirely untrue. He told me to wait and put down the phone while he went to get her. When she got on the line, I went to the point.

"Did Andrew mention anything, anything at all, about having met a white backer, someone who would finance a showing?"

"Hmm," she paused. "Actually, now that you mention it, he did. He said this man had stopped by the studio, and told him that he knew somebody, a man who owned a gallery downtown. The guy said he'd told this man about Andrew, and now the man wanted to see some of his work. But the guy was really busy during the day, so they decided to meet after hours one night this week."

"And who was this guy, the one who put him in touch with this backer?"

"I don't know. Andrew didn't say. Or if he did, I admit I wasn't paying attention. Why? Is it important?"

If I said, "Yes," she'd feel guilty. If I said, "No," she wouldn't have believed me. So, I said neither.

"Another question: Do you remember when you got there? What time it was?"

She reflected. "I left the house at about ten. It usually

takes me a half an hour to walk over there. So, it was about ten-thirty, I guess. Does it matter?"

"It could." I had one more question. "Has anyone contacted you, come to see you, to ask about Andrew's work?"

"You mean, looking to buy it?"

"Or put up a show."

"No. You're the only one who's been in here. I mean, there's still reporters coming by—I don't want to see them— and there's the lawyer you sent—he's real nice. Thank you for that. But nobody else. No, no one's been around asking about Andrew's work. Not a soul."

This confusion over the backer, I could sense that it was key, but I couldn't quite figure out how. So I decided to put it aside—for the moment—and concentrate on what I did know, did understand.

I spent the next few hours writing and revising. I finished three articles, including two detailed profiles, one on Andrew and one on Brandy. I described their hopes, their dreams, what made them special. Since Tessie was the target of so much speculation, the article on Andrew also included a good deal of information on her, as well as a recounting of their love story.

The third and longest article covered the investigation. I kept to the facts, but I admit to arranging them in a manner that highlighted the discrepancies in the case against her.

With great pleasure, I kept my word to Blackie and Kent, thoroughly lambasting the police and their knee-jerk focus on Tessie. I hit the cops for their lack of interest in Big Earl, a man known for his temper; and in his manager, with his ties to the mob and the mob's well-known interest in keeping colored boxers in their place.

I didn't stop there. I dragged some of the backstage characters out front and put them under a spotlight, namely the caller and the backer. Who were they? What did they know? Were they witnesses, or could one of them even be the killer?

The article mentioned the pictures of Brandy, but left out the salacious details, and questioned why the photos, if they were indeed the motive behind the killing, had been left out in the open, so easy to find.

I thought about mentioning the missing photo album, but decided against it. I'm not sure why. Some instinct, perhaps. What was important was that the article contained enough information—pointed to enough people—to show that there was a host of characters who could've pulled that trigger, and that Tessie was by far and wide not the only reasonable suspect.

When done, I stood, stretched and took a brief walk around the newsroom. Sam was working late. Most of the others had already gone. I thought about going into his office to talk to him, but changed my mind.

I still had work to do.

Back at my desk, I picked up my pencil and went over the profiles. Then I picked up the phone and put in a call to Mama King. I explained that I had written two articles that would be of interest to her and they were to come out in the next edition. She asked me to read them to her and I did. She gave me another quote for the profile on Andrew, one that I could also insert into the article on the investigation.

"The funeral's tomorrow," she reminded me. "I was hoping and praying Tessie could be there with me, but her lawyer—he's a nice man. Thank you for sending him to her—

he told me there's no chance the judge'll change his mind. Says he's already asked twice and he can't go back again."

"I'm very sorry, ma'am. I'm sure she'll be there in spirit."

"The important thing is for the people to hear the truth about my Andrew and who killed him. So, you keep working on that, you hear? You promise, you'll keep working on that."

After that, I called the boxing gym, hoping to catch Big Earl. One of the trainers answered and handed Big Earl the phone. I read him the stories. He actually thanked me for the call and told me that Brandy's funeral would also be on the morrow. It would take place in the morning, while Andrew's would be in the afternoon.

"Listen, you found out anything yet? You any closer to catching the mutherfu—" he caught himself, but not before I heard it, sensed it, felt it threatening to boil over and sear everyone it touched. Big Earl was choking on his own anger.

"Yes," I said, "I'm getting close. Real close. And it's bigger than I thought it was."

"Does that mean … what you said? About Banks and—"

"I was wrong. You're OK with him. You can trust him."

"Then who did it?" Big Earl demanded. "Who killed my baby?" His voice broke into a sob.

It hurt to hear him, to listen to that big man break down.

But he gained my respect. He did.

"Big Earl," I said softly. "Big Earl, listen to me. I just wrote an article. It … it throws dirt on a lot of people. You, included. You and Banks—"

"You did *what?* But why? You—"

"I'm setting a trap for the killer. Now, I need you to stay calm, stay cool. You got that?"

He didn't answer.

"Big Earl?"

There was a deep sniff and clearing of the throat.

"All right," he choked out.

"I'm doing all I can to find the answers. I can't promise you I will. Nobody honest can do that. But I promise you that I'll try."

More silence. Then a reluctant, "Thank you." A second later, he was gone, had hung up.

I stood there a moment, holding the receiver. *Promises. It's best never to make promises,* Hamp used to tell me. *Cause people never hear what you're saying, only what they want you to say.*

Feeling suddenly very tired, I put the receiver back on the hook, then leaned on the desk. I was sleeping badly these days.

You need a break, I could hear Hamp say.

Maybe, so, I agreed, *but when?*

His voice didn't answer.

27

The newspaper's morgue files, its archives, were down in the basement. Ethel Cane, the nonagenarian who oversaw the stacks, had arranged everything to her liking, using a system that only she understood. No one dared touch a stack or do any research without her assistance and say-so.

Experience had taught me that a bribe often helped smooth her prickly nature. So, I went prepared with a steaming hot freshly-brewed cup of joe.

"Just for me?" she said, accepting it with the graciousness of a queen accepting tribute. She took a cautious sip, tasted it, and gave a little nod. My little gift had been found worthy. She set it aside and gave me her attention. "You need my assistance?"

"Some information. This time on the disappearances of three little girls—"

"Two back in February, one this past summer?"

Nearly a century old and still had a mind like a steel file cabinet.

I followed her down the rows of archived newspapers, veered to the left, then down another row, and turned to the right, then down another two rows, and left again. It was mind-boggling. How could she keep it all straight?

But she did, and soon enough, I had three issues in my hand.

"Only three? I mean, it was three children missing. Are you telling me we only did three stories on it?"

"If the paper had done more, I would've given you more." She counted off her fingers: "One story for when the first two girls went missing; one for when one of them was found. And one for when the third disappeared."

"But there was at least one other development. What about when the last girl's bike was found?"

"What about it?" She raised an eyebrow. "No issue means there was no story. What can I say? Y'all blew it."

She shuffled away, muttering to herself, moving at a pace that belied her age. I had to hurry to keep up with her, knowing that if I didn't, I might be lost in those stacks forever.

She showed me to a small table set off in a corner with a lamp and reminded me of the rules—*her* rules—as though I didn't know them after hearing them dozens of times. No smoking. (Naturally.) No tearing the newspapers apart and leaving them a mess. (Naturally.) Put the pages back in the order in which I'd found them. (Ahem. I had never done otherwise.)

"And don't try to put the papers back yourself." She wagged a small thick index finger under my nose. "You people never get it right."

"Yes, ma'am," I said and gave her my solemn word.

* * *

The articles were thin, to put it mildly. They covered the barest details. Back in February, Dottie Hope and Janie Evans, both twelve years old, disappeared four days apart. The two girls had been playing ball together outside their apartment building on West 124th Street when the ball rolled off the sidewalk and down between two parked cars. Evans went to get it—and didn't come back.

The story stated that Hope didn't quite witness the kidnapping, but it also implied that she definitely saw something. When she disappeared just days later, police suspected that the kidnapper had come back to tie up a loose end. That suspicion appeared confirmed when a dog walker found Hope's body in Mount Morris Park, two days later, with a .32 caliber gunshot wound in her upper back.

A .32? It was the same caliber used in the King-Sullivan killings. And hadn't Thelma Lee said that the third girl's bike was found in Mount Morris Park?

I picked up the last article. It, like the others, was short and to the point. Back in July, Janet Johnson did what hundreds of mothers everywhere do every day: she sent her young daughter, Mildred, on a quick, last-minute run to the grocery store. Unlike those other girls, though, the nine-year-old didn't make it home.

The store was on 120th Street, only a block away from the Johnson home on 119th, just west of Lenox.

This third article did briefly refer to the Hope and Evans case, pointing out that Evans' body was never found. However, the article didn't outright connect the disappearances or voice any suspicion that the same person or persons might be behind them all.

There was no follow-up article and so no confirmation of Thelma Lee's statement about the finding of the Johnson girl's bike.

Including Cana, the missing girls were all of different ages. However, they all lived within or disappeared while passing through the same geographic parameters: Lenox Avenue to the west and Mount Morris Park to the east, 125th Street to the north, and 118th to the south.

I double-checked the bylines; they were all the same. Unfortunately, the reporter had since left the paper, so I couldn't speak with him to see if he had info that hadn't made it in.

Four Harlem girls kidnapped—and one murdered—in the space of a few months.

Thelma Lee was right. Someone was taking our children and, as far as I could tell, we hadn't done a thing to stop them. We hadn't warned the community or put pressure on the police to investigate.

That needed to change.

* * *

The boss was still in. I went past my desk, swept up my copy, then paused, thought about it and put the longest article, the third one on the investigation, back down.

I tapped on the boss's office door, opened it up a bit and stuck my head in. "Sam?"

"Hmm?" He looked up from the typed pages he was editing. "Yes?"

"I wanted to talk to you about another story I'm working on." I eased in but left the door ajar.

"Yeah?" he said, with faint annoyance, his brows furrowed.

I guess the expression on my face must've told him something because the expression on his changed.

"Oh, OK," he said slowly and gestured for me to take a seat. "What's up?" He laid aside his blue pencil and gave me his full attention.

I went in, leaving the door open a crack, and took a seat. First, I handed him the profiles on the King-Sullivan case.

"Is this all you have?"

"No. There's more. I just …"

"You just what?"

"I need to take another look at it."

"Well, give it here. That's what I'm here for."

"I know, but …"

"Lanie?"

"There's actually something else I wanted to talk to you about."

He laid my pages aside, his expression now full of concern, and nodded for me to begin.

I told him about Thelma Lee, her search for her baby girl and what she said about the missing children. He actually looked somewhat relieved when I was done.

"I remember the case of the two girls," he said, "but, tragic as it is, it—"

"It's part of a pattern, Sam."

"What makes you think that?"

"I checked our morgue files. There's something there, and I'd like to follow up on it."

"You're serious?"

"Yes, I am."

"Right in the middle of the King-Sullivan case? Does this mean you've given up on Tessie, cause if it does, your belief in her innocence or guilt shouldn't affect your interest in covering this story."

"No, no, I still want to—I still am—covering the King-Sullivan case. I am perfectly capable of covering more than one story at a time."

He leaned back and sighed. "The thing is, Lanie, the King-Sullivan business, that's right up your alley. The disappearances? That's not part of your normal turf."

"But I—"

"I only got management to agree to let you cover crime because I said it would happen only when it involved society players. Covering the disappearances of some little street kids would be—"

"An excellent use of my time. It would be doing what we say we're here to do, which is to serve the community."

He raised two hands in self-defense. "Remember, I am not your enemy. I'm on your side. It's just that—"

"She's poor." I dared him to deny it. "That's the only reason you've given me for not doing this story."

"Don't twist my words."

I got to my feet, leaned on his desk and gazed down at him.

"I am doing this story," I said. "And when I put it in front of you, you will read it. You may not like it—that's OK, because it's not a story to 'like'—but you will want to print it."

He teepee'd his fingertips, and studied me, a smile tickling the corners of his mouth. "Says you?"

"Hm-hmm." I said, straightening up and putting a hand on my hip. "Says me."

His gaze lingered on my lips. "Shut the door," he said, "and lock it."

"Why, Sam Delaney! I—"

"Then come on over here. We got some real talking to do."

* * *

We had a nice little private interlude, quick but satisfying. Afterward, I checked my hair, reapplied my lipstick, and went back to work. A few people looked up from their desks, but most didn't care. They had work to do.

I had to make one last phone call before heading out. It was to Blackie. It was just a quick call and it seemed to take him by surprise.

"You're *not* calling about the King-Sullivan case?" he asked. "No more questions about that anonymous caller?"

"I'm calling about something else entirely. A little girl. Her name is Cana Lee." I briefed him on my run-ins with

Cana's mother and the pattern I'd sensed when checking our newspaper morgue. "Do you recall the cases?"

"Not really. I mean, I hate to say it, but kids do run away—"

"Weren't you listening? At least one of these kids was found dead—"

"I know, I know. Look, I–I'll look into it. I can't promise you more than that."

It was less than I wanted but more than I expected.

"Thanks," I said, and hung up.

28

Twenty minutes later, I was back at the Fish 'n' Fry, sliding into my favorite seat. It was in a booth at the front by a window. Settling in, I laid my purse on the table and took off my gloves, but kept on my coat. It was warm in the diner, but not by much, especially so near the front door, where a chill breeze managed to sneak in.

I gazed out at the avenue, trying to organize my thoughts. On the short drive from my office, I'd realized the reason for my reluctance to turn in that last article. The fact was, I was pretty sure I knew the who and the how; I just wasn't sure of the why. If only I could figure out that last bit, I could finish my article and turn it in. A glance at my watch confirmed what I already knew, that a deadline was approaching and I was running out of time.

What had Kent said? That the killer was *cold and precise.* Images of the crime scene flashed through my mind and I was back there again, reliving the smell of blood, the glare of those camera lights, the ruined remains of what had been two living human beings only hours earlier.

Cold, precise—and ruthless. What had he been looking for?

That photo album? Could it have really been the—

A shadow fell over me, making my heart thud. Startled, I jumped, my hand going to my chest. I glanced up in a ridiculous panic, to find it was only Doreen standing there, holding my sandwich plate in one hand and a pot of coffee in the other.

"Thank you," I said, as she placed my food on the table and poured my coffee. "Darleen, what do you see when you look out there?"

She glanced at me as if to ask, "Are you serious?" A raised eyebrow told her I was.

"What do I see?" She shrugged, and looked out, past the rotating doors of the entryway.

"Nothing really. There ain't all that much to see. Especially not now, what with it being so chilly and gray and all."

She was right. At night, good weather or bad, the place was jumping, thanks to the clubs running along down the side streets, but this early in the evening, this little bit of a crossroad was as boring as boring could be. Could a picture of it have drawn a killer's ire?

"I heard that Andrew used to take pictures out there every day," I said. "You ever see him?"

"Oh, goodness yes." She bent slightly and pointed to the intersection just outside the entrance. "Right there. He used to stand his camera on that corner. He'd stand there and wait till he got the right feeling."

"The right feeling?"

"Yup. That's what he called it. The feeling that told him it was time to take that picture."

I studied the corner where Andrew had stood. Tried to see the world the way he'd seen it. What could he see while standing there? Who would have passed before him? And what had he noticed? What do you notice when you take up a position at the same spot, at the same time, day after day? Most regular folk might only notice the big changes because they're not paying attention—but someone like Andrew, he'd see the little ones, too.

Had he noticed a detail that had gotten him killed? Had he photographed it?

Thelma Lee walked by. She looked as tired as a long-distance runner.

I got up, stepped outside and beckoned her. "Come on in and rest your feet."

"I can't. I got to look—"

"I know, but you need a break. When was the last time you ate?"

She shrugged. "I don't know."

"Well, then."

I guided her to my table and asked Darleen to bring another sandwich and more coffee. Thelma started to object, but I waved her objections away.

"Thelma, I've decided to do that piece on your daughter."

Her face lit up. "Oh, you have?"

"Sure. Maybe you could just tell me something about her." I took out my pad and pencil and flipped to a blank page.

"You said she's been missing since last Saturday?"

"She left home to see the Lincoln Giants. You see, she's a bit of a tomboy, loves baseball and they're her favorite team."

"They were playing a doubleheader, up in the Bronx, right?"

"She got a ticket for her birthday. I should've gone with her, but I had to work."

Darleen brought the sandwich and coffee. Thelma took a quick sip of the steaming hot brew and then wrapped her hands around the cup to absorb its warmth.

"This is awfully kind of you."

"It's nothing."

She stared out at the street as if by looking hard enough, she could make Cana appear. "She's a real responsible girl," she said. "Knew her way home." She smiled sadly. "She was so happy when she got that ticket. Took her cap and ball. I remember watching her go out that door. She turned and said, 'Mama, I'm gonna get 'Pop' Lloyd to sign my ball. And I'm gonna tell him I got the prettiest Mama in the world. Maybe I can bring him home to dinner.' That's been our little joke. That one day she's gonna bring home a baseball player and I'm gonna marry him."

Tears welled in her eyes, but she blinked them back.

She was the last of her children, she said. Her two smallest had died of tuberculosis. "Sabrina was two and Linda was five." Her other girl had run away two years ago. She was fourteen. "I ain't seen or heard from Edie since. And now, Cana … But I know she didn't go 'way on her own."

I nodded at the plate. "Eat something."

She nodded, picked up the sandwich and took a small bite. For a few minutes, she was quiet, chewing, thinking.

"I know she didn't run off. I know something done happened to her."

"You say she knew the way home. Which way was that?"

She nodded out to the street. "She would've walked right past here, then on down the street, past the studio of that photographer that got killed the other day."

"She would've been walking south from the train station at 125th, right?"

"Hm-hmm. Then come on down, right past here."

"Where do y'all live?"

She pointed out to the street, then flicked her finger southward. "Just another two blocks away.

It wasn't hard to guess what she was thinking, that her child had nearly made it home. She was *just another block away.*

She put down the sandwich and pushed the plate away. "I'm sorry. I can't. I just can't. Not while she's out there."

"That's OK. But try to take care of yourself. You've got to keep your strength up."

"Why? What for?" Her gaze returned to the window. "Cana's my life. She's all I got left."

She pushed back her chair and took up her bag. "Thank you for listening, and for the sandwich, but I gots to go. I got about another half an hour before I go to work, and I—"

"I understand." I reached out to stop her. "One more question," I said. "You said 'she got the ticket.' Does that mean you didn't buy it for her?"

She shook her head. "No, it wasn't me. I ain't got no money for a ticket like that. Cana said a nice man gave it to her."

"Did he say who the 'nice man' was?"

She looked surprised at the question but considered it. After several seconds, she shook her head. "No, no, she didn't," she said, her forehead puckered with new worry.

"I promise you I'll write the story," I told her.

Her gaze went back out to the streets and her jaw moved with an expression that combined grief and resolve. She fished that sketch out of her bag and headed out. I watched her then looked over at the newspaper stand.

Soldier Jackson was sitting comfortably in his window, lightly juggling a baseball back and forth.

* * *

Tessie said she'd called the studio at nine-thirty. Gunshots were heard at ten, just about the time she was leaving home. She got to the studio at ten-thirty and found what she found. Five minutes after she walked through the door, the police got that anonymous tip.

My hand went to my mouth. How could I have made such a mistake? How could I have so overlooked the obvious?

I got up and hurried to the counter. "Darleen, this place doesn't have a phone, does it?"

"No, ma'am. But if you need one, there's one at the Rexall's on 125th Street."

The *Rexall's.* I hadn't even thought to go there when I was canvassing the neighborhood. And I should've. I should've been looking for where the tipster could've made that phone call.

It was the key to everything.

"I'll be right back," I said. Then I nearly flew out of that diner. Across the street, Soldier Jackson waved at me. I smiled and waved back.

Those three blocks from the diner to the pharmacy seemed to take forever. But it couldn't have been more than five minutes, with me dashing across the streets, crossing even with the red lights.

The payphone was just inside the front door. The man standing behind the counter had a clear view of it. I walked up to him and quickly introduced myself.

"Two nights ago, did anyone come in and use that phone? It would've been around ten o'clock."

He cocked his head, thought about it and nodded.

"You're sure," I said.

"Oh, yeah," he said. "I know him real good. He's always in here, buying medicine for that knee."

"Thank you."

I hurried over to the phone and put in a call to Blackie, only to have Sergeant Wilkins tell me that Blackie was out.

"Any word of when he'll be back?"

Wilkins said he didn't know.

"Tell him to get to the Fish n' Fry diner on West 122nd. Tell him I'm waiting there for him. I know who killed Andrew King and Brandy Sullivan."

"Sure, you do."

"Look, it's urgent, really urgent that he get my message."

"Yes, yes. I'll let him know."

Frustrated, I hung up.

* * *

Back at the diner, I ordered another coffee. The minutes ticked by. Five. Ten. There was a big clock on the wall behind the counter. I was looking at it every other minute. Across the street, Jackson was beginning to bring in his papers, put away his candy.

I glanced at the clock again.

Twelve lousy minutes had gone by and still no Blackie.

I thought about getting up, going back to the pharmacy and making another phone call. But suppose Jackson disappeared while I was gone?

I should've explained my full suspicions on the phone. I should've said it wasn't just a matter of Andrew and Brandy. That a life hung in the balance, the life of a little girl.

Fifteen minutes now. And Jackson was about to leave.

He locked the stand's side door and brought down the shutter, then set out.

I had a choice. Stay or go.

Suppose he *did* have Cana? Following him could be the fastest way to find out where Jackson lived and whether he had the girl.

I went to the counter and put down enough cash to cover the food, the coffee and a tip. When Darleen came to collect it, I told her that I'd sent a message to the police station for Blackie.

"Tell him I couldn't wait any longer. Tell him, I'm—"

At that moment, I saw that Jackson was leaving. I broke off in mid-sentence and ran out the door.

29

It was dark out now and had begun to drizzle. I turned up my coat collar and set out to follow Jackson, but from across the street. Walking parallel, and slightly behind him, I promised myself that I would just find out where he lived, then contact Blackie again.

Jackson walked with hunched shoulders, his hands shoved deep into his pockets, his stride uneven. *Arthritis*, he'd said and massaged his right knee.

I could imagine what had happened. There's Andrew, taking pictures of the same corner, every day, at the same time. He's become part of the background. He's such a common sight that it's easy to overlook him.

And that's what Jackson does.

The newspaper dealer, who prides himself on noticing everything, misses the one thing that's right under his nose. He even said that, didn't he? But with the girl's mother wandering up and down the street, he gets nervous. He starts worrying. He sees Andrew and panic breaks. Did Andrew take a picture of something that no one must see?

* * *

I kept a steady distance. Needles of rain pelted my hat and threatened to soak through my wool coat. I had begun to shiver, so I rolled up my fur collar as far as it would go and hugged it close. I told myself it wasn't really that cold outside, but I couldn't deny the creeping chill inside.

Jackson paused in a cone of light under a street lamp at the corner of 129th Street and I slipped into a store entryway. He lit a cigarette, cupping it against the rain, and threw a nervous glance over his shoulder.

The light changed. Jackson hobbled across the street, walking as fast as his arthritic leg would let him. I loosened the leash but kept him in sight.

* * *

All the time, my thoughts were churning, producing running images of the betrayal that must've gone down at the studio that night and in the days before. I could see it all: Jackson chatting Andrew up, telling him he knows someone who's got dough and is looking to patronize a young colored artist. He even offers to bring the man by that evening.

But *there is no white patron*. When Jackson shows up, he's alone.

Maybe, he says he wants to see Andrew's work before he recommends it. So, Andrew agrees to spread his latest album out for Jackson to see. Maybe, he's just developed the pictures from the last few days and hung them up to dry. Maybe, he hasn't even had a chance to examine them, since he's had pictures for paying customers that were due.

He goes into his darkroom, takes out the dried prints and starts to add them to the album. He pauses over one picture, struck by its significance. Now, he knows why Jackson wanted to see the collection, but it's too late.

He turns to find Jackson holding a gun on him. Then the bell over the front door tinkles.

It's Brandy, come to get her pictures. Andrew's upset, but

he knows he's got to take care of her. He begs Jackson not to hurt her.

Just let me give her her pictures. I'll get her out of the shop.

Jackson nods but warns him not to try anything. He'll be watching. He motions Andrew forward, follows him to the front of the shop and stands in the shadows, watching.

Andrew welcomes Brandy, engages uneasily in some small talk. He tries to make everything appear normal, but he's desperate to get her out of the shop. And so, he makes a mistake. Or maybe Jackson's so paranoid that he decides he can't afford to let her live. Andrew's about to hand Brandy her pictures, when Jackson steps out of the dark, his gun held high. He forces them both to the back, and there he puts them both out of business, permanently.

* * *

Jackson paused at the steps to a narrow townhouse on 128th street, the first house on the corner.

I stepped into the well of a store entrance and watched as he patted his pockets, looking for his keys.

A curtain at one of the windows on the second floor twitched and a small face peered down at Jackson. The distance from where I stood wasn't all that far. I narrowed my eyes and a girl's face came into focus. My heart leaped.

Cana?

But how could I be sure?

The curtain slid closed and the face melted back into the darkness. Meanwhile, Jackson, having apparently found his keys, was limping up the stairs, in a slow but steady climb.

"Hey, Jackson!" I stepped from the store entryway and called out, raising my voice to be heard over the din of the traffic and the rain. "Jackson!"

He didn't respond. I made to run across the street, but the light changed and a tidal wave of cars surged past, forcing me back onto the pavement. Across the street, Jackson fiddled with the lock on his building door. I readied myself to dash across the street the moment the traffic eased up.

"Hey, lady," said a voice next to me, "you'd better watch out. You could get killed that way and I don't feel like seeing somebody die today."

It was a newsboy. I glanced at him just long enough to gauge his age—around twelve, maybe thirteen, wearing a worn coat, a cap with a hole, torn knickers, and soaking wet. Then my gaze went back to what was happening across the street.

Jackson had stepped inside and was shutting the door behind him.

"Listen," I told the boy. "I need your help. Get to the cops. Go to the station on 135th Street. Ask for Blackie. You got that? *Detective* Blackie. And tell him that Lanie Price sent you. Tell him I need him. That you saw me, here."

His young eyes were older than his years. He nodded toward the house across the street, the one he'd seen me staring at. "You sure you should be going in there? Maybe you should just wait."

"I can't." My gaze returned to the house, to that second-floor window. "There's a man in there and he's got a little girl."

"His kid?"

"No, he's kidnapped her. Girl's mother's been looking all over for her."

His eyes widened. "You mean that lady? It's *her* kid? I mean, I seen her asking around and—" Something clicked and his shock died under a dark understanding. He looked at the house. "Shit," he muttered. "So, it's like that, huh?"

"Yeah, it's like that."

The light changed and the traffic slowed to a halt. "I've got to go. Promise me—"

"I know. Detective Blackie. And you're Lanie Price."

I dug into my purse, and pulled out a couple of loose dollar bills. "Here's something for your trouble."

He grabbed the cash—"Don't worry 'bout it. I'll get your man down here, fast."—and took off running, his thin legs pumping.

* * *

According to the labels over the doorbells, he was in Apartment 23. I buzzed other apartments until someone let me in. Opening the door, I stepped inside and hit a wall of stench: a mixture of mildew, beer, maybe old food and definitely busted toilets. A long hallway painted in meconium green and dimly lit by a lonely bulb, stretched out ahead, telescoping to a stairway at the far end.

I headed toward it, my thoughts in a whirl. What would I say to Jackson? How could I explain my breaking in on him?

I paused at the foot of the stairwell, heart pounding. Could I trust that newsboy? Would he keep his promise? Something about him had struck me as dependable. There are times when your life depends on instinctive decisions made like that. Was this one of them? I decided I was going to have faith in the kid. No choice, really. I just had to hope and pray that when he got to the station, those cops would take him seriously and Blackie would be there.

I put a hand on the railing, but then yanked it back. The banisters were grimy and sticky. I started up. The steps, originally of pale stone, were stained, dirty and cracked. The air grew heavier and harder to breathe with every step.

Pausing on the second-floor landing, I took a moment to pat my hair and compose myself. What would I do once I got in there?

If I was wrong about everything, then it would be OK. Jackson would be surprised at seeing me, but he wouldn't feel threatened.

But suppose I was right? What would I do?

Every instinct screamed, *Walk away!* Instead, I took a deep breath, headed down the hall, found Apartment 23 and knocked.

No answer. Only silence. I knocked again. More silence. Then came the sound of the latch being undone. The door swung inward and Jackson stood there. The room behind him was in shadow. He had removed his wet hat and coat, and stripped down to a dingy shirt. A toothpick dangled from one corner of his mouth. Seeing me, he leaned on the doorway with his left arm. In his right hand, he held a .38, down low.

"Well, Lady Lanie, what took you so long?"

His voice was a lazy drawl. The toothpick bobbed up and down as he spoke.

"I hear you've got company," I said.

"Sure do." He grinned. "Come on in." He stepped back "We been waiting for you."

I stared at him, at the dull, flat aspect in his eyes. Snake's eyes. Ruthless, without mercy. The smart thing would've been to walk away, to have never gone there in the first place.

But I had, and now, I went in.

30

J ackson kicked the door shut, slammed me against the wall and pressed his forearm against my throat.

"Put your hands up." His heavy breath buffeted my face, thick with onions and garlic.

Taken off guard, I hesitated. He jammed the sharp nozzle of the gun into my cheek. I cringed and put up my hands.

"You packing?" he asked.

I shook my head. He ripped the purse out of my hand, thumbed open the clutch and dumped the contents on the floor. My lipstick and compact, steno pad and pencils, as well as some loose coins, a thin wallet and keys clattered to the floor.

"You see," I said, heart pounding. "No gun."

He dropped the purse and kicked it away. "Turn on the lights," he said.

For a moment, I was confused, wondering whether he was talking to me, but then I saw movement in the shadows. A small table lamp came on and a little girl stepped into the spill of light.

She was thin and frail. Tear-streaks marked her grime-smudged cheeks. Dark circles rimmed one large, terrified eye. The other eye was shut, swollen with an ugly purplish bruise. She was a mere ghost of the girl in the sketch, and barely recognizable. But it was her, all right.

It was Cana—Cana Lee.

* * *

Jackson jammed his gun in my back and prodded me toward a wooden table and two chairs in a corner next to a window. "Sit," he said when I hesitated.

I eased myself down onto the chair that had its back to the wall and placed my hands on the table, where he could see them.

"Anybody know you're here?" he asked.

"I sent a message."

"To who?"

"The cops."

He let out a bark of laughter. "Seriously? Why'd you bother? The police don't care nothing 'bout you and me— and they sure don't care nothing 'bout *her*." He gestured to Cana.

The girl had retreated to the false safety of the shadows, to huddle on a mattress on the floor in a corner. The mattress, like everything else in the place, looked pitiful and filthy. It was soiled and stained and I didn't want to think about what kind of stains they might be. No, I didn't want to think about what this child had endured, what Jackson might've done to her. I just knew I meant to get her out of there, away from this twisted son-of-a-bitch, and back to where she belonged, in her mama's arms.

I forced myself to breathe normally, and to think. This was a one-room apartment. There were only two ways out: the door to my right and the window to my left. We were on the second floor and there was no fire escape, so no way out there. That left the door. And that meant going through—or around—Jackson. But how? Even with a bum knee, he was bigger and stronger, and he had a weapon to boot.

I took in the rest of the place. What could I use if the opportunity arose? The place was spartan. A black coal stove to cook on. A sink attached to the wall. A dark brown dresser stood on the other side of the window. It held a rectangular mirror, set leaning against the wall. There was also a single glass and a bottle of hooch.

So, Jackson drank here alone.

Next to the bottle were toys: a small stuffed animal, a primitive dollhouse, and a colored Raggedy Ann—toys to lure a child. To get her to lower her guard and trust a man who couldn't be trusted.

"Like what you see?" Jackson looked amused, as if he could read my thoughts. He turned the other chair around and eased down on it. Resting his arms on the chair back, he pointed the gun at me.

Outside, the rain beat against the windowpane in a staccato *ratta-tat-tat*. Barely visible through a slit in the curtains, the bright lights of the big city were reduced to a dull, charcoal blur, with smudges of red, orange and blue. I'd only been in this room a few minutes but already found it stifling. This place was a prison and we were locked inside it, Cana and I, with a man who wouldn't hesitate to kill us.

There had to be a way out. There had to be. I just didn't see it.

Not yet.

"Me and the girl," he said. "We had a nice thing going. Why'd you have to go and mess it up? Come here? Follow me? Why'd you have to stick your nose where it don't belong?"

"She should be home with her mama. She wants her girl back."

"Does she now?"

"Remember how I told you the paper's offering a reward for her return? You can collect it."

"How much?"

I thought quickly. The amount couldn't be too high or too low. It had to be just right. Had to be … realistic.

"Five C-notes," I said.

His jaw dropped in surprise. "Five hundred—for *her*?"

I shrugged. "OK, then. If you don't think she's worth it— If you don't think *you're* worth it—we could pay you less. How about two-fifty?"

For a moment, he didn't seem to get the joke. Then he did, and burst out laughing. "Lady Lanie, you got nerve."

I glanced over at Cana. "Her mother's got friends."

"Yeah, right."

"You'd be surprised."

"Well, I guess I would." He leaned forwarded. "So, tell me about this money, about how it's gonna come to me."

"All you have to do is let us go."

"Is that right? Just let you … and the girl … walk on outta here."

"You're afraid I'll call the cops."

"No, cause you said you already done that."

"But I didn't tell you why I called them. I just said I needed help. As a matter-of-fact, the message was that *you* needed help."

His eyebrows shot up. "Me?"

"So, you see. It could be perfectly fine. All you've got to do is just—"

"Let you and the girl go."

I nodded.

"And I can trust you to keep your mouth shut?" he asked.

"Shut about what? All I know is that you found a missing girl. That's all it's been, right? You found a missing girl?"

"Yeah," he said. "That's all it's been."

"You found her and then I found you, and told you who she was."

"That'll be the story?"

"If you want it to be."

Several seconds passed. He studied me, his lips curved in a small ugly smile, his eyes cold and measuring. Then he twisted round in his chair, and beckoned Cana. The girl got up slowly and came over. She seemed very weak. Jackson put a heavy arm around her thin shoulders, yanked her close and whispered loudly in her ear.

"This lady here, she said she wanna take you away from me. You want to go with her?"

Cana kept her head bowed, but her gaze flickered up to meet mine. Hope battled fear. I gave her an encouraging little nod, and for a moment there, I thought—

But then Jackson tightened his grip, and the girl dropped her gaze. Visibly trembling, she shook her head.

Not satisfied, Jackson gave her a little shake. "What'd you say? I didn't hear you. Speak up, girl. You wanna go with her or stay here and get more loving from me?"

Cana licked her lips and spoke in a small, careful voice. "I–I want to stay here, with you."

"And do what?" Jackson pressed. "'Get more loving.' Say it. 'And get more loving."

"And ... get more loving."

Jackson turned to me with a smug smile. "See? She don't wanna go nowhere."

He whispered something in Cana's ear, and the girl cringed. Jackson gave her a loud, wet kiss, spun her around, and gave her a swat on her backside. Cana flinched and hurried back to the corner.

Jackson turned to me, "The thing you don't understand is that she don't just like me. She *loves* me. And I love her. I'm good for her, way better than that damn Thelma Lee ever was. Why, she let her out on that street, to walk by herself. I wouldna never done that."

"No, you'd keep her prisoner here."

"Y'see." He wagged a finger at me. "I knew it. I knew you was one of them people, one of them high and mighty dicties. Y'all don't understand nothing."

I leaned forward. "All right, then. Make me understand. Tell me why a grown man would abuse a child like that."

"I don't have to tell you shit."

"No, you don't. But I'm the only one who's going to be standing between you and those cops."

"Oh, you mean the ones who ain't never gonna show up?"

"They'll be here."

As if on cue, the sound of sirens came from a distance. Faint, but clear. Jackson tensed, his expression tight. And we all held still.

The sounds grew, swelling ever louder, ever closer. I dared feel a sense of relief. They were right beneath our window.

And then they weren't.

They had passed us by. Soon, it became clear that this rescue was not meant for us. Soon the sound of the sirens faded completely and all we were left with, once again, was the pounding of the driving rain. My heart sank, even as Jackson's apparently lifted.

"You see?" he said. "You can stop listening. Stop waiting. There's always sirens going off in this neighborhood."

"True. But soon they'll be coming *here*, for *me*—me and that girl. And it's going to be up to me to tell them whether you're the devil—or a saint."

His nostrils flared.

"Why, Cana?" I pushed. "Why do that, to this child, *any* child?"

"Why? Why *not?*" He exploded, jumping up, the

movement so violent it knocked over the chair. "I was alone. Understand? Alone. Every damn day, alone. But *she* was there. And she *saw* me. Not like the others."

He paced back and forth.

"What others?" I asked.

"The others," he said bitterly. "The ones who come by every day. They toss me that chicken scratch like they throwing change to a beggar. Don't even bother to look me in the eye, treat me like I'm a fucking ghost, invisible."

I recalled the man who'd tossed him the coins for the newspaper while I was standing there, recalled Jackson's anger. I had thought it disproportionate, but I hadn't realized its significance.

"But Cana was different?" I asked.

"Hell, yeah! She *saw* me. *Spoke* to me. She *liked* me. Understand? She *liked* me. I could see it. And she ... well, she was alone, too. Her mama was never there. But *I* was. And I knew what she liked, what she wanted, what she *needed*. Love. A *man's* love. So, I used to talk to her. Most every day, I'd talk to her. She'd stop by my newsstand, tell me about school, and we'd talk about baseball. I always made sure to have something for her."

"The baseball ticket. That *was* you."

"Yeah," Jackson smiled. "She even stopped by afterward to thank me." He glanced over at Cana with a look of deep affection. It was astonishing, how mercurial he was, how swiftly he could move from one emotion to the other.

"And then?" I prodded, as much to turn his attention away from Cana as to get him to continue his story.

"And then ... I brought her here."

That chill came back, and along with it anger. He'd had Cana here for days now, days in which he'd watched Thelma Lee seek desperately for her baby.

"Have there been others?" I asked.

He stopped his pacing. His breathing sounded heavy in the silence, like an animal in a lair. "Three," he said finally.

Three.

"And did you let them go?"

He didn't answer.

"After ..." I paused, trying to find the right words. "Afterward–after you finished with them, did you—"

"What do you think?" he said in a voice tight with anger. "You think I was gonna send them back to *those* people, those people who didn't even know how to love them? They was mine. They *belonged* to me. And they *wanted* to stay with me."

The chill settled into my bones. "So ... what happened to them? Where are th—"

"Here," he said. "With us. With me." He stared past me, to a point over my shoulder. I turned and followed his gaze—to the wall behind me.

The cold set in deep, chilling my bones.

31

Seeing my expression, he burst into laughter. He pointed at me and started to speak, but laughter overcame him.

He doubled over, drunk with hilarity, holding his stomach and clapping his hands.

"You really believed me. Good grief, woman, I ain't crazy. All that talk about burying bodies in my walls? You can't believe that. Cause if you did ..." He straightened up, suddenly sober and deadly serious, "there'd be no way I could let you go."

He paused to let those words sink in and sink in they did, like stones weighing down a body in a lake. Then, he arched and twisted to stretch his back. Walking over to the dresser, he slipped the gun under his belt in the curve of his spine. He poured himself a drink and tossed it back, staring at himself in the mirror.

I caught movement out of the corner of my eye. It was Cana, crawling across the mattress, creeping toward Jackson. She was going for the gun. I shook my head, warning her against it.

Jackson said, "Don't try it, girl. I can see you in the mirror."

My heart thudded. Cana froze, then scurried backward. She squeezed herself into the corner. Knees bent, she covered his head with his arms against the blows experience must've taught her to expect, turning herself into a small, tight, terrified ball.

Jackson nodded, his eyes on Cana's reflection. "That's a good girl. You stay like that. Y'hear? You stay just like that, till I call for you."

Cana whimpered a reply.

"What did you say?" Jackson said. "I couldn't hear what you said. Did you insult me, girl?" He set the glass down and flexed his fists, ready to deliver a brutal blow.

"She said she was sorry," I interjected. "That's all. She said she was sorry."

Jackson's eyes slithered to my reflection. "Did she now?"

"Yeah," I met his gaze. "She did."

For an instant, I wondered whether I'd gone too far. I do think that, for a moment, his instinct was to lash out—the spark of anger showed clearly in his eyes—but for some reason, he chose differently. He chose to smile.

"You know, I like you. You don't back down. But one of these days, Lady Lanie, one of these days it's gonna get you killed."

That false smile disappeared. He downed the rest of his drink and poured himself another. For several long seconds, he stared at my reflection in the mirror, sizing me up, measuring me.

"You know, don't you?"

His voice was low, his tone casual, but the words themselves sent a jolt of fear through me.

"Know what?"

"That I did it."

It was stupid, but I played dumb. "Did what?"

He rounded on me with cold fury. "Don't play games with me, bitch. I know you didn't come here 'cause of that girl. And you sure ain't called no police on account of her. No, you're here ..." he paused grimly. "You're here cause of Andrew."

I didn't answer. I had not planned on mentioning Andrew. I didn't want Jackson to know of my suspicion. The way I saw it, the more he realized I knew, the more likely he was to kill us. I held my breath, unsure how to answer.

Turns out I didn't have to. The drink had loosened his tongue; he kept right on talking.

"I betcha didn't know," he said, "That me and Andrew, we was in the war together."

I said nothing.

He poured himself another one, drank half. "Sounds crazy, but them were some of the best days I ever had, them times in the war. We was respected, y'know? We was *some*body—even *he*roes." He swirled the liquid in his glass, studying it. "Well, some of us was. Not me, of course, but some of us."

"You mean, like Andrew?" I dared speak, recalling the medal on Mama King's wall.

"Yeah," he laughed bitterly. "like him." He shook his head. "That man, that man ... hmph, hmph, hmph. He was a hero— and a fool. Actually," he paused, "we was all fools. Heroes, my eye! We thought—we *actually* thought—they would see us that way. When we come back, we thought it was *all* gonna be different. Cause we had proved ourselves, our worth to this country."

He shook his head. "But didn't nothing change. All that bleeding and killing and dying. It was for *nothing*. It didn't change a thing, not a damn thing. If anything, it just made it worse. Cause we come back proud. No! We come back uppity! So, Mr. Charlie, he had to put us in our place. To remind us of what we are and where we belong—right under his fucking heel."

I remembered that summer when the troops came home. Harlem was so proud of its doughboys. It was the summer of 1919, the Red Summer, they would come to call it. The streets Down South flowed with the blood of lynched colored soldiers—American soldiers killed by Americans on American soil.

But Andrew's death wasn't a case of lynching. This was something else entirely.

Jackson looked over at me, his eyes bleary and now bloodshot. "When did you know? How'd you know?"

I took a moment, judging which approach to take. My guts told me it would be best to keep him talking—and reveal as little as possible about what I knew.

"You and Andrew," I began, "how'd you end up doing business across the street from one another?"

My question appeared to surprise him.

He paused, thought about it, gave a little shrug. "Fate, I guess. We ran into each other one day. He said he was gonna open up a studio, invited me to drop by. I said I would, *but* ..." He gave a wry smile. "You know how it is. You say you will, but you don't never really mean to."

"But you did, stop by?"

"Yeah," he sighed, "I did. One night, I just said, 'Why not?' Truth was, I'd heard everybody talking about it. The King Studio. They was all saying how fine it was. What a great picture-taker he was. So, one day, I just sorta slid on by."

"And?"

"I liked the place. It looked nice, real nice, and I told him so." He took another drink. "Then what?"

He licked his lips. A look of shame—shame and

resentment—flitted across his face. "Well, I guess he asked me how I was doing. That's what."

"And?"

"Well, hell, it was obvious. I wasn't doing so hot. He didn't have to rub my face in it, to make me say it. My old lady had left me. Said I was no good. That I couldn't keep a job. Fact was, I couldn't *find* one. Not a decent one. Was I supposed to put up with the way they talked to me? Looked down at me? Called me 'nigger'? Hell, no!"

"You're bitter."

"Damn straight I am!"

He turned on me defiantly, giving me a hard stare. I stared right back, and after a while, his ire gave way to a lopsided grin.

"Sister, you really don't back down, do you?"

I slowly shook my head. "No, I'm not known to." I gestured toward his glass. "Now, how about you give me one?"

"*You* … a drink?"

I nodded.

He let his mouth fall open in mock shock, then closed it again. "Well, forgive my manners." He adopted a Southern accent. "I do apologize. I just didn't think a lady like yourself would—

"Well, the lady would. Thank you."

His grin ripened into a smile. He actually danced a little jig as he poured and brought the drink over to me, danced as much as that bum knee would let him.

The stuff smelled so strong, it stung my eyes. But I smiled gamely, even clinked glasses with him. The glass would make such a good weapon. I could see myself smashing him over the head with it. Together, we offered a toast to unsung heroes, and then I asked what had happened next.

"What happened?" he repeated, frowning and mulling it

over as though it was the most profound question he'd ever been asked. Perhaps, it was. How do you go from considering someone your friend to seeing him as your enemy, and killing him in cold blood? Maybe, he hadn't thought about it before. Maybe, he'd successfully managed not to.

He was silent a long, long time, but eventually started up again.

"Andrew said the block was a good place to have a business. That it had lots of people walking up and down it, all times of day and night. There was a newsstand across from his studio, he said, and the old guy who had it wanted to sell it. The guy was tired, had been doing it for way too long and wanted to get out. 'Is that right?' I said. 'How much you reckon he want for it?' Andrew said he didn't know, but that I should go over and find out. So, I did. But ..."

He looked away.

"Well, of course, I didn't have the coin for it." He paused. "Andrew should've known that. I tried to tell him, but he wouldn't listen. Had to rub my nose in it."

He sucked his teeth, his expression bitter.

"But, obviously, you *did* find the money," I said. "I mean, you ended up with the newsstand."

"Course, I did. My good friend Andrew, he made sure of that. He *fixed* it for me." His voice dripped with sarcasm and resentment.

"Fixed it how?"

"What do you mean how? I'm telling you he fixed it for me! That's all you need to know! He fixed it."

So, Andrew had lent him the money, or outright given it to him.

"He was a good man," I said, watching Jackson closely. "A good friend."

"Maybe. Maybe, not." Something flickered in Jackson's eyes. "Fact is, he owed me."

"Really?"

"Yeah." He gripped his glass, his face tight.

I said nothing, knowing he wouldn't be able to hold it in.

"I saved his life. You didn't know that, did you?"

I didn't answer, didn't have to. The liquor had him on a roll—that and a guilty conscience.

"Yeah, I saved his ass, all right. Damn straight I did." He downed the rest and wiped his mouth. "Damn straight."

He stalked back over to the dresser, poured himself another, then turned and leaned against the dresser for support. The strong drink was already making him less steady. He looked over at me, saw that my glass was still full.

"Hey, you ain't drinking. I wouldna given it to you if I'da known you was gonna waste it."

"I won't," I said, thinking about exactly how and when I meant to use it. For appearance's sake, I took a sip and forced myself not to grimace. It was bathtub gin, pure poison. "Delicious."

"Aww, you's a lady," he laughed. "Ladies don't drink."

This one does, I thought, *just not this stuff.* It was the worst moonshine I'd ever tasted—and I've done my share of tasting.

"You were saying?"

For a moment, he looked blank; then he remembered and his expression darkened.

"It was back in the war. We was in a jam, a bad one. Me and Andrew, we was sent out to scout the enemy's position. Andrew lost his nerve. Was talking crazy 'bout deserting. I was trying to talk him out of it, when this big old Kraut, he come out of nowhere, went straight for Andrew. If it hadna been for me, that muthafucka woulda got him. I mean that was one big muthafucka, but I pulled his ass off Andrew and gave that Kraut the what-for. But in the fighting I got hurt. Hell, that's how I got this bum knee. Saving his sorry ass.

Andrew, he come out of it without a scratch. And when they found us, they just assumed he was the one done the saving, the protecting. But it was *me* done that. *Me!* Not nobody else! *I'm the one* done saved that nigger's ass.

"Matter of fact, I saved all they lives that day. Turns out that Kraut was some sort of commander and shit. When his troops saw what I done to him, they turn tail and run. You hear me?! I saved a lotta lives that day. A lotta lives. Me! Not him. *Me!*" he thumped his chest. "It was *me* who saved the *he*ro; *me* who sent them muthafuckas a'running. *ME*—not *him.*"

His chest heaved and he blinked back angry tears.

"I see," I said gently, sympathetically. "*You* were the real hero, but *he* got the medal. You were brave *and* generous. You let him take the credit."

"Yeah," he nodded. "I did. I didn't tell nobody how he wanted to run. All these years, I done kept my mouth shut. I kept it shut."

"You kept his secret. All these years, you kept it, but ..."

He studied me, his expression bitter. "Go on."

"When it was your turn, he wouldn't keep yours. Right? He wouldn't keep your secret. Is that what happened?"

He raised his glass to his lips, but then saw that it was empty and set it down. He picked up the bottle, but apparently it was empty, too. He gave a long sigh, and slowly sagged down into a squat, his back against the dresser. He looked around, wearily, then closed his eyes and rested his head against the dresser.

"I didn't mean to do it, but ... I had to. He saw me. Had a picture of me. Didn't even know he took it. Not till he developed it. Just happened 'cause of that stupid project of his, where he was standing on the corner, day in, day out, every damn day. Said he was gonna take that picture to the police. I said I'd let the girl go. He said it was too late, that people like me needed to be stopped. Said he was gonna have a little girl one day and that if somebody like me ever touched her, he'd kill him."

Jackson was indignant. "How d'you like that? He complained about *somebody like me,* when I'm the one who saved his damn life."

And you're the one who eventually took it.

Jackson looked at me with eyes begging for understanding.

"So, I had to do it. Had to. He didn't give me no choice. After all we been through, he pushed me up 'gainst a wall like that. Didn't give me no choice."

"And what about Brandy?"

"That dancer? Oh, she just happened to be in the wrong place ..."

"At the wrong time."

"Well, yes and no. Andrew was trying to get her out of the shop, and I was gonna let her go, but then I thought about it. Killing her made everything easier. So, I got 'em to go in the back. Then I shot him through the eye, her through the mouth. I figured the cops would think she'd killed him, then did herself. Or, they'd think it was the mob. Everybody knew that Big Earl was throwing fights, that Brandy was against it. She was talking too much. Everybody knew that."

"Either way, it was a good game of misdirection."

"That's right. I was thinking on my feet. I always been good at that." He smiled, but then his expression changed. "But you know, I got to say, I'm a little sorry 'bout having to shoot that pretty dancer gal. But it was her or me, just one of those things. Now, if it hadda been Tessie. If she'd a been there, I woulda been happy to pop her one."

"That's right. You don't like her."

"Ain't nothing there to like. What a bitch! She hated me

the minute she laid eyes on me. Wish it was her I killed, 'stead of that dancer."

"Well, then how *did* Tessie get caught up in all this?" I asked, waiting for him to confirm my suspicions.

"Don't you get it? I saw her go in, and it came to me. I knew I could fix her, but good. Call the cops and let 'em find her there. Knew they'd be happy to slap the cuffs on her."

"So, when Tessie showed up, you decided to call the cops and get, shall we say, another layer of protection?"

He grinned. He liked that. "Yeah. That sounds about right."

Outside the rain had let up, but it was still gray and cold. I studied Jackson. He was still lying. How to get him to admit the truth?

"Your friend Andrew is dead, Jackson. Don't you miss him?"

He drew a deep sigh and nodded with drunken regret. "Yeah, I do. But he made me do it. I was just gonna go in there and find that picture, but then he showed up and that dancer came in right after. I didn't have no choice then, did I?"

"Oh, but you did. Because Andrew didn't just show up. You arranged for him to be there. You made up that story about a rich man being interested in his work. Told him you'd set up a meeting for that night."

A lazy lopsided grin slowly widened his mouth. Drunk or not, he knew I had his number.

"You sure are something, Lady Lanie. Too bad I'm gonna have to kill you."

So, we were back to that again. "Now, why would you want to do that?" I heard myself ask. The words came out as though they belonged to someone else and sounded a whole lot more confident than I really felt. The fumes of that noxious drink must've been getting to me.

He chuckled. "'Why?' she asks. Why? Maybe, it's cause you could get my ass sent to jail."

"How?"

He started to speak, but I hushed him.

"I mean, really, think about it," I said. "If I say one thing, you can say another. Who are they going to believe? A lowly woman like me or an ex-soldier man like you? It would be my word against yours."

He looked surprised, considered the thought, and nodded. "Yeah. You got that right." He motioned to Cana. "But what about her?"

"Well, you know if they don't believe me, they're not gonna believe her. It's like you said: Who cares about a little colored gal?"

"Well, your paper does," he said. "You said it put up a reward for her."

"Sure it did. But that's kind of like advertising."

He wrinkled his forehead. "Advertising?"

"Hm-hmm. People hear you're willing to pay that kind of fancy dough for information, they know the story's important. They buy the paper to read it."

"Oh, I see. You mean the dough's not real. It's just—"

"No, no, no! It's real. Oh, honey, is it real! And it could be all yours. All you gots to do is—"

"I know. Let you and her go." He sighed, closed his eyes. "Boy, what I could do with heavy sugar like that! First thing, I'd buy me a steak, and a fine suit, and then a fast car."

"It could be yours. All yours."

He opened his eyes, looked at me. "You sure?"

"I'm sure—"

Another tired sigh. "Well, then, I guess … if you're sure now, then … OK."

I couldn't believe it. I couldn't believe my ears. "OK?" I repeated. "We can go?"

His head bobbed up and down. "Yup. Dang me for a fool, but I'm letting you go. Trusting you now, to—"

My heart lifted as though it had been freed from a ten-ton weight. Yes, yes! I opened my mouth to seal the deal, when I heard it—a sound, one I would've welcomed only a short while ago.

He raised a finger, turned his head toward the window and listened.

"You hear that?" he asked.

Sirens. In the distance, but quickly approaching. And this time, they were headed for us. I knew it. I could feel it.

"No," I said. "I don't hear anything."

He was instantly sober. He gave me a look that clearly said he didn't believe me. I wouldn't have believed me, either.

We both leaned forward, tense.

Closer. Closer. They were coming closer.

I looked at him and he looked at me, as though we were comrades in this together. But we weren't, and we knew it. There had been a moment of trust. One in which we'd reached a tentative agreement. But that moment was gone. If it was the cops downstairs, Blackie to the rescue, then Jackson and I were back to square one, and all bets, all agreements, were off.

We waited. For a moment there, I forgot to breathe and seeing his face, I think he did, too.

No mistaking it now. They were headed our way.

Then they stopped. We exchanged another glance. They were there, right there, under the window. Then, the sirens died, leaving a void of deafening silence.

32

Bright beams lit up the window and a booming voice, thick with an Irish accent, filled the room.

"Roscoe Jackson, this is Detective John Blackie. With the New York City Police Department. We got yer house surrounded. We hear you've got two of me friends in there. We expect you to let them go and come out with yer hands up." His Irish accent had come out, as it did in times of stress.

Jackson shot to his feet, grabbed the gun from the dresser top and crept up to the window. He eased up to one side, drew back one of the dingy curtain panels and peered out.

His eyes widened and his nostrils flared at the sight before him. One of the light beams slid across his face, illuminating it with a harsh glare. He hissed and pulled back, a vampire caught in the light of day.

Blackie's familiar voice, multiplied by a bullhorn, came again.

"Jackson, I saw ya and I know yer can hear me. So, listen here. I want yer to come out and come out now."

Jackson looked over at me, his eyes ablaze. "You did this."

Blackie's voice boomed again. "I won't be waiting much

longer. I'll be coming in and coming in shooting. 'Course I don't want to do that. I want to see everybody come outta this alive. But if you don't give me some sign that my friends are OK, I'll have no choice, but to—"

Jackson turned to me. "Come over here, bitch."

I rose to my feet, careful of making any sudden moves.

He pointed his gun at Cana. "Move! Or she gets it. Now!"

I moved from behind the table, skirted past the turned over chair. Jackson grabbed me and shoved me in front of the window. Then he dropped down, pushed up the lower window pane. I gasped at the sudden blast of cold wind and rain.

The street below was ablaze with the headlights of police cars, all of them swiveled to point at this window. I spotted Blackie, holding a bullhorn and staring up at us, his face grim.

Jackson jammed the nozzle of the gun up against my temple and positioned himself directly behind me.

"Now, listen here," he yelled. "I got a pistol on Lady Lanie, here. You make one move and I'll give it to her—but good."

"No tricky moves, lad. I promise you. I'm thinking we can help each other out here. First, just let me hear from the lady herself."

Jackson ground the gun against my head. "Speak, but don't get no fancy ideas."

"Blackie?" I yelled down. "It's me, Lanie. Cana's here, too. Cana Lee. And we're OK."

I could see Blackie's face well enough to discern his anger and worry. His dark bushy eyebrows knitted together and his jaw clenched. He gave me a silent nod.

Jackson said, "Tell him to back off."

"They just want to talk."

"Don't shit me. Tell them to back off."

"They're not going to do that, and definitely not just 'cause I say so."

"I thought you had a special connection with the coppers. You telling me you don't? Cause that would be too bad for you." He pressed the gun harder against my head.

"I'm telling you they're not going away."

"Jackson?" It was Blackie. "You can still walk away from this—*alive.* All yer gotta do is let 'em go. I repeat, let 'em go—unharmed—and I guarantee ya, I promise you—"

"Promise me what?" Jackson yelled. "Don't try to give me no line. I give 'em up and you guys'll give me a lead coffin. I ain't no fool. She's in here and she's staying in here—long as I say so."

Jackson slammed down the windowpane, then edged backward, holding me as a shield. When we were far enough away from the window for him to feel safe, he shoved me away.

I stumbled and fell, then hurried onto the mattress to sit next to Cana, who curled up next to me. She was thin, so thin. I wrapped my arms around her.

"Jackson!" Blackie called out. His voice was muted by the closed window pane, but still distinct. "Jackson, talk to me!"

"Jackson," I said. "If you don't talk to them, they're going to come in blasting. That's just how they are."

"Shut up!"

"Please! Listen to me! They're going to shoot first and ask questions later. We could all get killed. Cana, too. I thought you—"

"Shut up! SHUT UP! You gotta let me think!"

He covered his ears and paced back and forth. Cana and I sat huddled together, watching him. Minutes crawled by.

Blackie was still shouting outside, calling for Jackson to come back to the window. He was losing patience and I didn't blame him, but I wished he'd calm down. His worry was making me scared, more scared than I'd been before. I'd meant it when I said we could all get killed. All it took was one cop who didn't know what was what. All it took was a couple of stray bullets to find the wrong targets. In the barrage of gunfire that followed when cops cut loose, both the innocent and the guilty could die.

And Jackson had to know it. Every resident of Harlem knew it.

From outside came the bullhorn again. "What's going on in there? Jackson? I'm giving you five seconds to get to this window, or I'm coming in."

That did it. Jackson stopped his pacing and came and stood over us. He wasn't that tall, but he seemed to tower over us. He stared down at me, then dropped down on his haunches, and put his face close to mine.

"Lady, you got guts. I gotta admit it. You really do. But you gonna need more than that—a lot more—to get outta here alive."

He yanked me up and dragged me to the window. He opened it and I braced myself against the winter-like gusts that swept in.

"You want 'em?" Jackson yelled. "Well, I want something, too. A car, a fast one. And twenty large. I want twenty large—in cash, old bills. And, oh, yeah. A steak. I want a steak, piping hot, with all the fixings. You got that?" To me, he hissed: "You think they gonna do that? Get together all that to save you and that girl?"

I grit my teeth and stayed silent.

Blackie's voice boomed back, sounding unexpectedly cordial. "A car and twenty, huh? You've got expensive tastes there, laddie. Very expensive tastes."

"You gonna do it or not?"

"I guess we're gonna have to. Them's the conditions you set, right?"

"Right."

"Of course, you know I'm gonna need something in return."

"You want her?"

A pause, then: "We're going to need the girl. Nothing happens without the girl."

Jackson whispered in my ear. "I guess there's your answer. You don't mean nothing to him." To Blackie, he yelled. "It's a deal. You got thirty minutes."

"We'll need more time than that."

"OK. Thirty-*five*, then. You got thirty-five minutes. If you're not here with my car, my money, and my food, in thirty-five, then Lady Lanie here and this kid, they both gonna die."

"But, that's not enough time. I can't guarantee—"

Jackson shut the window, cutting Blackie off in mid-sentence.

"Well, I sure showed him," he said. "Now, they know who's the boss here, that I'm in control."

I guess he didn't like the loud silence I gave him for an answer. He shoved me toward the table, told me to, "Sit down and shut up."

Then he went back to pacing, beset by a restless energy.

Watching him, I tried to keep my nerves in check. I kept telling myself to be relieved. I had nothing to worry about. A deal had been struck. The child would be free. That was the important thing. After that, who knew? But I needn't worry. Blackie would look out for me, too.

Jackson returned to his place in front of the dresser and slid down on his haunches. He checked his gun, slid it under his belt, took it out again and rechecked it.

Minutes ticked by. They crawled by. Ten, fifteen, maybe twenty. I got tired of trying to reassure myself. I was worried. Of course, I was. I had every right to be. I didn't trust Jackson. How could I? For that matter, I couldn't trust Blackie, either. Not with something like this. Goodness only knew what he was actually planning to do.

Jackson must've been thinking the same thing. He wiped his face with his hands, stretched his legs out and sank down on his butt. He closed his eyes for a time and drew a deep and weary breath.

Cana tensed, looking like she was about to make a move, but I shook my head. *No, don't.* Even with the cops outside, it was too risky.

Jackson moaned, opened his eyes and turned his gaze on me. All of his mad energy was gone. He looked tired, resigned. All the bravado he'd had when talking to Blackie had left him.

"They gonna kill me dead, ain't they?"

I didn't bother to respond. The answer was obvious. I glanced over at Cana, wishing I could hold her, comfort her —and if necessary shield her with my body should the cops burst in.

Jackson straightened up with a sigh and got to his feet. He shoved the pistol under his belt in the curve of his back, went to the sink and ran some water in his glass. He took one gulp, then spat it out and threw the rest into the sink.

"Gonna get me some real liquor when I get outta here," he muttered. Then, he turned to me, saw the glass on the table.

"Hey, wait a minute. You still got your drink—"

Blackie's muffled voice pierced the window. "Jackson! Jackson, we've got what you wanted! Come to the window. Now!"

Jackson rushed to the window, parted the curtains and looked out. He was in such a hurry, he didn't bother grabbing me for protection.

"We've got the dough and the car," I heard Blackie say.

"What about my steak?"

"We got that, too. But it's gonna get cold mighty quick. Now, I've kept my promise. I need you to keep yours. The girl. Send out the girl."

Jackson's nostrils flared. "No. We gonna come outta here together. And if you try anything, I'll take them down with me. You can bet on it."

He was so busy defying the cops he didn't see what I saw, not till it was too late.

33

I didn't dare move a muscle, not even shake my head, for fear it would catch Jackson's attention. Silently, Cana crept up behind him. The girl moved as silently as a cat, as quickly as a ghost, until she was well within arm's reach.

Then she yanked the gun out of Jackson's belt and stepped back.

"What the fu—?"

Jackson whirled around, patting his lower back for the gun, then straightened up to see Cana aiming it at him.

"What the hell you think you doing?" Jackson stuck his hand out. "Gimme that. Give it on back, y'hear?"

The girl's hands were trembling. Her eyes shimmered with tears.

"Jackson?" Blackie's voice blared.

I came from around the desk.

Jackson put up a hand, stopped me. "Don't you dare."

Blackie was calling out, again and again. "Jackson? Jackson? What's going on in there? Lanie? *Will somebody answer me?!*"

"Cana, get out," I said. "Now's your chance! Go!"

"Shut up!" Jackson rounded on me, fist raised, ready to strike.

"No, don't!" Cana cried. "Don't you hurt her!"

Jackson's nostrils flared hard, but he halted. He swung back around and glared at the girl.

"Now, listen here. If you know what's good for you, you'll gimme that gun."

He took a step toward the girl.

Cana fell back a step, but she kept the gun raised high.

"Cana, please," I begged her. "Go! Get out, now!"

"You don't even know how to use that," Jackson said. "You ain't got the *guts* to use it." He advanced another step. "Come on! Shoot me, baby. Shoot me! I dare you."

Cana broke out in a cold sweat. Beads of perspiration dotted her forehead. She bit her lower lip.

Jackson edged closer and closer, teasing her, taunting her. "You just a dumb young heifer, ya hear? You ain't got the guts to shoot me."

Cana was trembling so badly, she couldn't keep the gun still. It was visibly shaking.

Jackson lunged and knocked the gun aside. Cana cried out as Jackson smacked her. Cana went down, the gun went flying and Jackson lunged for it. I jumped onto his back and tackled him.

"Cana, run! *Run!*"

Jackson was broad and strong, but that knee of his was weak. It gave out under my weight and we tumbled to the floor in a heap.

"Cana, now!" I yelled. "Get out!"

I disentangled myself and scrambled for the gun. Jackson grabbed me by the ankle, yanked me back, and flipped me over onto my back. He straddled me, wrapped his thick hands around my throat and squeezed. I clawed at his hands and pounded on his arms, twisting and turning uselessly under his weight.

"Stop!" Cana cried. "Stop! You're hurting her!"

Jackson's bloodshot eyes were lit with maniacal intent. His grip around my neck tightened. I flailed at him, trying to scratch his face, but I couldn't reach him.

"You made me do this," he whispered between clenched teeth. "You *made* me. It's your fault."

He leaned downward, putting his weight behind it, as his thumbs pressed on my trachea.

"No," I rasped and managed to rake his cheek with my nails. But by then, the room was spinning and my vision was going fuzzy. I was weakening and my lungs were crying for air. Screaming for air. Darkness crept around the edges of my vision.

Through a haze of agony, I heard the deafening explosion of a gunshot. Something hot whistled past and slammed into the wall behind us. Then came another explosion. Warm liquid spattered my face and the grip around my throat slackened. Jackson arched and his eyes went wide, so wide, and his mouth opened in shock.

Bam! Bam-bam-bam!

His body jerked again and again, doing the dead man's dance. Then I heard a chamber click empty and Jackson slumped forward, to land on me, heavy and suffocating and inert.

For a moment, I lay stunned. Then I pushed him off me and crawled away. I got to my feet, gasping for air and massaging my throat.

Jackson lay face down in a spreading pool of blood, his eyes and mouth gaping open. Cana stood holding the smoking weapon, her small hands welded around it. My first thought was that the cops would be there any minute.

"Put it down, honey," I said and held out a hand. "Please. Put it down."

She was as still as a statue, staring, unblinking, at Jackson. I edged closer, still speaking softly, but she didn't respond. I put my hands on top of hers and pressed them downward.

"Honey, it's OK, now. You can let go."

I tried to unlace her fingers and remove the weapon, but they were frozen in place.

"You can let go," I whispered.

Suddenly, her chest heaved and she gasped as if coming up for air.

"I didn't want to," she whispered. "I told him I didn't. I told him. I told him I didn't want to—"

Her face crumpled; her hands opened and the gun clattered to the floor. Tears slid down her cheeks.

"Oh, God," I kicked the gun away, dropped to my knees and put my arms around her. She slumped against me and I enfolded her in my arms, holding her close. She sobbed, her small frame shuddering, her face buried in my fur collar.

"I didn't want to," she kept repeating. "I told him ... I told him I didn't want to."

Silently I prayed, thanking God for our safety, and telling Cana what a brave girl she'd been and that everything would be OK, that soon she'd be back home, safe.

I looked over at Jackson. He was no longer a threat to us. His days of killing and kidnapping and molesting were over.

I felt anything but relieved.

That bleeding hunk of meat represented my last hope of saving Tessie. What would I do now? How would I prove that Tessie was innocent and that the dead man was guilty?

That's when I heard it, the earthquake rumbling down the hall.

34

The door burst open, kicked in by a horde of cops. They surged in, guns drawn, with Blackie in the lead.

I held out a hand to stop them. "It's OK. We're OK."

Blackie looked from me to the girl and the body on the floor. "We heard shooting. What happened?"

"I'll answer all your questions later, but right now this girl needs to be taken away from here. She needs to go back home to her mama. Right now."

"But—"

"I said I'll tell you everything. But first her."

Blackie nodded. He flicked a finger and a uniform stepped forward. The officer put a hand on Cana's shoulder, but the girl flinched and clung to me.

I hugged her tightly then slowly loosened her grip and held her away. I covered her little hands. They were ice cold. "It's OK. You can go with them. They'll take you home."

"No. I—"

"Hush, now. It's gonna be OK."

She hesitated.

"Go on," I said. "It'll be all right."

Cana looked up at the cop and let the man take her hand and lead her out the room.

Another cop called out from behind me, "I think this man is still alive."

Stunned, I hurried across the room and dropped down by Jackson's side. The cop had rolled him over so that he now lay on his side. Blood trickled from a corner of his mouth, but he was indeed still breathing. Blackie holstered his weapon and knelt down next to me.

"Jackson," I said, "tell them. Please, tell them. You got to say it for the police to hear. Admit that you killed Andrew and Brandy."

Blackie looked at me in surprise. "Is that true?"

I nodded. "Andrew saw him with the girl," I explained, then looked back down at Jackson. "Please," I said softly.

He coughed up blood and gazed up at me, that wry grin tugging at his lips. "You'd … you'd li … like that … wouldn't you? You'd … you'd …" Then his voice faded, his lips relaxed and his eyes slid closed.

Blackie put a firm hand on Jackson's shoulder and gave it a little shake.

"C'mon man. I can tell you're still with us. But from the looks of it, you won't be for long. Do you want to take such a sin to your grave? Tell the truth and save your soul. Did you do it? Did you kill those two?"

Jackson's eyes fluttered open. He gasped. His eyes met mine and his chin moved up and down. The movement was barely perceptible. It could've been the result of his labored effort to breathe. But I thought it was a nod in response to Blackie's question.

It was all Jackson gave. He arched, gulping for air. His mouth opened and closed, opened and closed, as though he was trying to speak, but nothing more came out, nothing but a bubble of blood. He closed his eyes and seemed to sink into himself.

"Jackson," Blackie shook him. "Jackson." But he was gone.

Blackie sat back on his heels and pushed his hat back, contemplating the dead man.

"Did you see?" I said. "Did you see?"

Blackie looked up at me. "See what?"

"That nod. He nodded before he died."

Blackie stared at me in disbelief. I looked him right in the eye, daring him to disagree. He rubbed his forehead and shook his head in doubt.

"I don't know, Lanie. I—"

"It was. A deathbed. Confession," I said firmly.

Blackie pressed his lips together in a fine, tight line.

I started. "He—"

Blackie held a hand up. Several seconds passed. Finally, he sighed. "All right, yes." He said in a tired voice. "A deathbed confession, it was." He got to his feet.

"You saw it."

"I saw it."

"And it'll be enough? Enough to set Tessie free?"

Another silence. Then a curt nod. "I'll talk to the DA about it."

I started to speak, but he held up a hand again.

"I'll talk to the DA and I'll put some weight behind it. I can't promise you, anything, but yes, after what I've seen here, I think it'll be enough."

35

But, as it turns out, Jackson wasn't gone. He was still alive. He was taken to Harlem Hospital, where the surgeons worked a miracle; Jackson regained consciousness the next day. He found himself handcuffed to his bed and Blackie waiting to see him.

Blackie talked to me later that morning. "Jackson was groggy from all the painkillers. But he was aware enough to understand what I told him. I had to explain that he had confessed, that he had made a gesture that indicated an admission of guilt in the homicide deaths of Andrew King and Brandy Sullivan, and that as a result, the district attorney's office was considering murder charges against him.

"Well, he denied it. He denied it all. From the deathbed confession to everything you said he told you. We either misunderstood him, he said, or you outright lied."

"What about him saying that he'd done this before, to other children, that he had their bodies buried in—Just search his apartment. You'll—"

"I can't! Don't you understand? It's a he said-she said right now. We have no proof. His claim that you lied pulls the rug out from under our feet. We have no good legal reason for going in there."

I couldn't believe this, didn't want to believe it. "So, Tessie's—"

"Back where she started. In jail. Facing murder charges. Again, without that confession, there's no evidence to charge him."

"And what about the kidnapping charges? What about what he did to Cana?"

"The girl's scared witless and so's her mother. She won't let the girl testify in court, won't even bring charges. She doesn't want her reliving the nightmare, she said, having to tell strangers what he did to her. The mother said just wants to move on."

I sighed. I could understand her feeling like that. God knows I could. But we just couldn't let a man like Jackson go free. He'd just do it again. I thought hard.

"What about the part where he held me at gunpoint? You saw him do that. You saw him standing with me at the window."

"True. Sort of. I didn't see the gun. That's point one. Point two: if we charge him in holding you, then we'll have to get into why you were there in the first place."

"And that would mean mentioning Cana, getting her name in the papers ..."

"And making her appear in court."

I drew a deep breath. "So, Jackson's going to get away with it—all of it."

"Looks that way."

"And you can't do anything about it?"

"My hands are tied. The mother won't charge him in the kidnapping. The D.A. won't charge him in the murders."

I thought about it, about what I could do, if anything. "I'd like to go in and talk to him."

Blackie was skeptical. "Sure. Why not? But it's up to the hospital, and up to him. I certainly won't try to stop you."

* * *

Jackson was propped up in bed. He shared the room with five other men. I drew the curtain to give us privacy.

"Looks like you're going to live."

"Hm-hmm." He was smug. "They say they took out three bullets. I am one hard-to-kill muthafucka."

"Yes, you are." I took him in from head-to-toe. "The hospital cleaned you up a bit."

"Yeah, I almost look respectable." He gave a little chuckle, then grimaced in apparent pain. "So, I take it you're here to apologize for what you and the girl did to me."

"For what we did to you!" I started to lay into him, but then caught myself and kept my tone sweet. "Now, why would you think that?"

"Cause I thought you mighta been served already."

"Served how?"

"My lawsuit. I'm suing you."

"You're *what?*" There, I must admit, my tone slipped a bit.

"I done spoke to a lawyer. He says I got a good case. I'm suing you *and* the girl, for assault."

There were a lot of things I wanted to say to that, but I restrained myself. All I said was, "I see."

"So, if you not here about *that,* then why are you here?"

"Oh, nothing major. I just wanted to check up on you— and introduce you to Big Earl."

"Big Earl?" He gave a surprised frown. "Ain't he the ..."

"The prizefighter. And the husband of the woman you killed."

I smiled and enjoyed the way fear entered his eyes.

"Wha-what you want to bring him here for?"

I shook my head. "Oh, no particular reason. He said he'd like to meet you."

"Meet me?" His gaze darted behind me. "He here now?"

I nodded. "Standing outside your hospital door."

He licked his lips. "I don't think I'm up to it today."

"That's all right." I gave him a firm pat on the shoulder. "I told him that might happen. And you know what he said? He'll be waiting for you when you get outside."

Message delivered. Message understood.

Jackson gave me a venomous look. "You're a bi—"

"I know. I know. But the fact of it is: I got your number—and now so does he."

* * *

Not an hour later, Blackie called me. "What did you say to him?"

"Who?"

"Why, Jackson, of course. What did you tell him?"

"Me? Nothing. Absolutely nothing. Why?"

"Because he's suddenly changed his tune. He's practically demanding we arrest him. He's confessed all over again, to the murder, the kidnapping, everything. Says he *wants* us to put him in jail—where he'll be safe, he said, from you—and Big Earl."

"Well, I don't know nothing about that."

"Did you tell him that Big Earl was going to kill him?"

"Of course not. I haven't seen or talked to Big Earl since Jackson was arrested."

Blackie paused. "You're sure about that?"

I smiled into the phone. "I'm sure."

36

B lackie and his men raided Jackson's apartment two hours later. Police recovered the missing photo album.

They also found hollowed out areas in the walls and, inside them, the remains of the two missing girls, Evans and Johnson.

Meanwhile, the funerals for Brandy and Andrew were held at the Abyssinian Baptist Church, Brandy's in the morning, Andrew's in the afternoon. Adam Clayton Powell served as pastor for both.

Tessie got her to wish, to be there at Andrew's funeral and say good-bye to the love of her life. She stood side-by-side with Mama King, the two women holding one another.

Tessie told me later, "I'll be here for as long as Mama King wants me, and I hope it's for a good long time."

The DA charged Jackson in the murders of Andrew King and Brandy Sullivan, and separately in the deaths of Evans, Johnson, and Hope. Tessie and Mama King attended the proceedings, were there in the deathly still courtroom to hear Jackson plead guilty.

Surprisingly, Big Earl was not.

To be honest, it stunned me to hear Jackson confess to multiple murders, kidnapping, and child molestation—all of which normally led to a death sentence—just to avoid a confrontation with Big Earl. What happened later helped clarify matters.

It seems he viewed a tangle with Big Earl as a definite death penalty, whereas he thought he wiggle room with the state, room to negotiate.

He cut a deal. He'd been killing, it seemed, for a long, long time. He offered to close other cases, to show where the bodies were. The community protested, but the DA agreed.

In the end, it didn't matter.

Hours after Jackson arrived in Sing Sing, he was found dead in the prison shower. The killers had broken every bone in his body and taken their time doing it. Some murders are quiet. This one wasn't. The sound of fists and iron bars pummeling flesh and cracking bone, the killers' grunts, and the dying man's screams must've carried. Yet, the guards and prisoners who'd been nearby said they didn't hear a thing.

Word had it that Big Earl arranged it. Police made a half-hearted attempt to investigate but didn't really bother. Privately, I revised my opinion: Big Earl might've been cool-headed enough to kill at a distance, after all.

Soon afterward, the prizefighter moved to Marseille, where he opened a restaurant, *Chez Brandy*. It soon became a sensation, dishing out New Orleans shrimp gumbo, fatback, and collard greens.

Back here in Harlem, Teddy Banks succeeded in closing down the Cotton Club—for all of five days—as Madden outmaneuvered the feds again.

As for Andrew's legacy, it turned out he had used the stove in his office as a makeshift safe. He had packed it with photographic plates and prints, made for his project. Nella introduced Andrew's work to Colin Radcliffe, owner of the Radcliffe Galleries, down on Christopher Street. He fell in love with Andrew's work and mounted a very successful exhibit.

I purchased one of the prints.

It still hangs over my desk—a picture of a bald-headed man, his back to the camera, as he walks down the street with his arm around the shoulders of a young girl.

ENJOYED THIS BOOK?

You can make a difference.

Leave a review at Amazon.com. On your favorite website. On your blog. On Facebook. Anywhere. Everywhere. And recommend my books to your friends.

Reviews are the most powerful tools in my arsenal when it comes to getting attention for my books. Much as I wish I did, I don't (yet) have the financial muscle of a New York publisher.

But I do have you.

Your opinion matters. It counts.

The more reviews my books receive, the more visible they remain. Just a couple of sentences will do. Even one sentence would be great!

Thanks a bunch!

ABOUT THE AUTHOR

"Just the facts, ma'am. Just the facts."

Persia Walker writes critically-acclaimed 1920s crime novels. A native New Yorker, she has lived in Germany, Brazil, and Poland. She loves Indian food and lives with her extraordinary cat, Sunday. Her online home is persiawalker.com. You can connect with her there or via Messenger on Facebook.com.

facebook.com/authorpersiawalker
amazon.com/author/persiawalker
instagram.com/persiawalkerbooks

ALSO BY PERSIA WALKER

Have you read the others?

Goodfellowe House

Lanie Price will go anywhere, talk to anyone, to get her story. So when she revisits the unsolved mystery of a young woman's disappearance, she starts asking questions—the right questions, but of the wrong kind of people. Come along as Lanie adds sizzle to this cold, cold case.

Black Orchid Blues

Lanie Price witnesses the brutal nightclub kidnapping of the "Black Orchid," a sultry, seductive singer with a mysterious past. Hours later, a gruesome package lands on Lanie's doorstep, but with an address that points to someone else. She soon finds herself elbows-deep in a mystery in which everyone seems to have a secret worth killing for.

Backdrop to Murder

For Lanie Price, the photographer found shot through the eye in the back of his studio is more than just another story. It's personal. On a dank night in September, Lanie is called to the scene of a grisly double murder. The victims: a popular photographer and a Cotton Club beauty. The suspect: the dead man's jealous wife. The cops say she did it and an outraged community believes it. But when Lanie delves deeper, she finds much sinister forces at work.

Lyrics of a Blackbird

Civil rights attorney David McKay disappeared years ago while investigating a lynching. Now, he's back, very much alive and determined to find the truth behind his sister's brutal death. His search rips back the curtain on the glittering world of the Harlem Renaissance to reveal a world of lies, hypocrisy, and tragic betrayal. Each day brings him closer to the truth—and closer to ruin. How soon before time runs out? How soon before his enemies uncover his own secret shame—the sin that could destroy him?